To: D

MW01120943

The
Fossil
Hunter of
Sydney
Mines

Jo Ann Yhard

Hope you enjoy the read!
It's pretty different from
our work life, isn't it?

Your friend
Jo!

☺

NIMBUS
PUBLISHING

Nimbus Publishing Limited
PO Box 9166
Halifax, NS B3K 5M8
(902) 455-4286 www.nimbus.ca

Printed and bound in Canada

Design: Jennifer Embree
Front cover illustration: Gerry Cleary
Author photo: Rhonda Basden

Library and Archives Canada Cataloguing in Publication
    Yhard, Jo Ann
    The fossil hunter of Sydney Mines / Jo Ann Yhard.
    ISBN 978-1-55109-760-2
I. Title.   PS8647.H37F67 2010   jC813'.6   C2009-907321-8

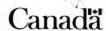  

The Canada Council | Le Conseil des Arts
for the Arts | du Canada

NOVA SCOTIA
Tourism, Culture and Heritage

We acknowledge the financial support of the Government of Canada through the Book Publishing Industry Development Program (BPIDP) and the Canada Council, and of the Province of Nova Scotia through the Department of Tourism, Culture and Heritage for our publishing activities.

This book was printed on
Ancient-Forest Friendly paper

ANCIENT FOREST
FRIENDLY™

For James, my best friend and sounding board. For Mom, who gave me the nudge and helped me find my path. And for Mary, my buddy and fellow explorer.

Chapter

I

GRACE DOUBLE-CHECKED HER GEAR: FLASHLIGHT, MATCHES, pocket knife, caving rope, rock hammer, and gloves—all there. She grabbed her trusty Dalhousie University baseball cap. Her thoughts flipped back to the day her dad had given it to her. She squeezed her eyes tight and tried to stop the memory from coming. The strategy usually worked, but not this time. It had been three months ago, on her birthday—the worst day of her life.

That morning he'd made her favourite breakfast, blueberry pancakes.

"Here's part one of your present," he'd said after she'd blown out the candles on her pancakes and they'd eaten so much they could hardly move. He'd pulled out a baseball cap that was embroidered with the letters *DAL*, short for Dalhousie. It was identical to the one he'd worn every day. He had earned his doctorate in geology at Dalhousie and she was going to do the same.

"I love it," she'd said.

Then he'd left for work with his trusty fossil bag over his shoulder, just like every other day. It had seemed so normal, but it was the last time she'd ever seen him.

She had anxiously waited for him to come home that night. There had been a knock on the door and she'd run to open it. Her smile had quickly faded as she stared in shock at two police officers.

Her mother had sent her upstairs.

Shore Road. Car crash. Ocean. No body. The words had drifted up to her as she huddled in her room.

Now, as she packed her fossil-hunting gear in her bag, she felt the sting of tears, just as she had that fateful evening. Shaking her head, Grace tried again to rattle the memory to the back of her brain—into that dark corner where she locked away all those memories. This time it obediently returned to its hiding place and she sighed with relief.

KCHHHHH!

Grace's walkie-talkie squawked loudly. It must be Fred, finally. She'd told him to radio her as soon as he got home.

"Fred, come in," Grace said into the walkie-talkie. Within seconds, there was an answering crackle.

"Roger, Grace. Fred here."

"Radio Jeeter and Mai. Tell them to meet us at Black Hole in thirty minutes." Grace paused, trying to calm her stuttering heartbeat. "It's an emergency!"

"What's going on?"

"I'll fill you in later. Get moving, okay?"

"Sure thing, Grace. Over."

Grace flung her battered backpack over her shoulder, grabbed her hat, and raced out the door. "Darn," she muttered, making a U-turn back into the house. She ran to the kitchen counter and scribbled a note for her mother:

Gone to Jessica's to study. Math test. Back by nine. Yes, I ate already. Love, G.

This should cover my tracks for a few hours, Grace thought. A shiver of guilt rippled through her as she re-read the note. Well, it wasn't a total lie. She *had* eaten already. She slapped the note on the fridge and headed out the side door. Of course Mr. Stuckless was watching from his window.

"Hi, Mr. Stuckless!" Grace waved and gritted a smile at their next-door neighbour as she passed by his window. *Nosy old goat*, she thought, backing her bike out of the garage. *He must be stuck to that window. He probably has a portable toilet under him so he never has to move!* She hopped on her bike and coasted slowly down her driveway.

She picked up speed and was soon flying down Queen Street. Without a thought, she took her hands off the handlebars to put on her hat and reached up to tug her long blonde ponytail through the back of it. Hands dangling at her sides, she thought about what had happened that day. Her head was spinning. Who could have done it?

Playing the day back in her mind, she tried to remember the last time she'd been at her locker. Had there been anyone hanging around? She couldn't say for sure, but she didn't think so.

Grace was so lost in thought as she zipped down Pitt Street that she nearly missed the turnoff. Checking behind her to make sure no one was watching, she veered past a pair of rusted gates with a faded danger sign and onto a forgotten path that ran through an overgrown field called the heaps. Gangly alders and tall elephant ear plants immediately hid the streets from view.

She cycled slowly and scanned the ground with her eyes, always on the lookout for sinkholes. They could appear anywhere, even here in the fields where the old coal wash plant used to be.

Perched above a spiderweb of coal seams at the edge of the Atlantic Ocean in Cape Breton, the town of Sydney Mines had a labyrinth of coal mining tunnels—both commercial and illegal bootleg tunnels—running beneath its surface. The commercial mines were hundreds of metres deep and stretched for kilometres out under the ocean, but they had been shut down for many years. They had been flooded with sea water long ago. The bootleg tunnels were usually shallower, and often ran directly from miners' backyards into the coal seams. As the years went by, the miners had kept digging under their homes, making longer and wider tunnels to extract more coal. For many of the poverty-stricken residents of Sydney Mines, illegal mining had been the only way they could heat their homes and survive. The tunnels were long since abandoned, their coal extracted. Some of them had collapsed.

Coal also meant fossils and there were plenty of those in Sydney Mines too, if you knew where to look. Grace had been a fossil hunter practically since she could walk. Back then her dad used to call it hunting for dinosaur bones. He would take her to Lachman's Beach, where it was flat and sandy. She'd found her first fern fossil there. Her dad had chipped it out of a large piece of broken slate with his rock hammer. Grace had proudly donated it to the fossil museum when it first opened.

Several years ago, Grace had taken Mai and Fred to the museum to show them all the fossils she'd donated. As soon as Fred had seen her name on the "Donated by" plaque, he'd decided he wanted to have his name on a plaque too. They'd been fossil-hunting together ever since.

Grace, Mai, and Fred had found this perfect clubhouse last year. They'd been cutting across the heaps one day, when Fred had almost fallen in a sinkhole. The hole had been created by the earth collapsing over an abandoned bootleg mine. When they'd climbed down to investigate, they'd been amazed to discover tunnels at the bottom they could walk through.

Before they found Black Hole, Grace and her friends' fossil hunts had been above ground at places like Lachman's Beach, Florence Beach, Sutherland's Corner, and the old strip mine at Halfway Road. Exploring the bootleg mining tunnels that were connected to Black Hole was way more exciting than hunting for fossils along the beaches. Many of the bootleg mines stretched all the way under the town. But rooting around in illegal caves was much more dangerous than fossil-hunting on the beaches. Grace knew it; they all did.

Ducking behind a huge oak tree, Grace hid her bike behind some foliage and skidded down a nearby bank. At the bottom of the slope was a pile of old lumber. Grace carefully moved the pieces of wood aside, revealing the hidden entrance to Black Hole.

Grace turned on the electric lantern she and her friends kept at the entrance and soon the inky walls of the mine were bathed in a soft glow. Deeper in the cave she could see the outline of the logs they had set up as benches and the rough wooden table they'd made. Fossils and other treasures they'd found on past expeditions were tucked in scattered hollows of the cavern walls.

As Grace waited for her friends, the sounds of water gurgling in the brook that ran through the hideaway and the slow drip of water trickling down from the ceiling were the only noises interrupting the silence until—

"Ouch!"

"Good grief, Fred. Do you have to hit your head on that log every time?"

"Come off it, Mai. It's not *every* time."

Grace sighed in exasperation. "Will you guys keep it down?" she frowned at her bickering best friends as they entered the cave. "It's supposed to be our *secret* headquarters!"

"Well, blame Fred—he makes such a racket," Mai said, brushing dirt from one of the logs before perching daintily on its edge. Her smooth caramel skin glowed in the shadowy light.

"Where's Jeeter?" asked Grace.

"He said he'd be here later," Fred replied, tossing his pack on the wooden table with one hand and hauling up his baggy jeans with the other. "I told him to come right away, but he didn't seem too worried about it."

"What's the big rush?" Mai asked. "Fred said it was an emergency, but I figured he must have been exaggerating, as usual." She tucked her shiny black locks behind her ear and threw Fred a playfully mocking look.

Grace grinned at Mai. It was so easy to get Fred going—it had been ever since they'd all become best friends a hundred years ago, way back in grade three.

Fred muttered something about not being appreciated and began digging around in his backpack. His chunky build and round cheeks were telltale signs of his favourite hobby: munching on chocolate. He pulled out three bars and tossed one to Grace.

She tossed it back. "Allergic to peanuts, remember? One bite and I'd be barfing my guts up."

"Oops, sorry," he said, grabbing another. "So what's going on, Grace?"

Grace's face turned serious as she ripped open her chocolate bar wrapper. Tension bubbled back to the surface as she answered. "You're not going to believe this!"

Mai leaned forward. "What?"

Grace tossed a piece of paper onto the table. "I found this in my locker today."

Mai gasped and Fred's mouth stopped mid-chew as they read the note:

Chapter

2

"IT WASN'T AN ACCIDENT? DO YOU THINK THAT HAS SOMETHING to do with your dad?" Mai's brown eyes blinked in surprise.

Fred squirmed, looking troubled. "But Grace, it's been almost three months since the car crash. Who would leave a note after all this time?"

"What else could it mean?" Grace jumped up from her seat. "It never made sense—that he didn't come right home that night, and that they never found...him." She paced back and forth, chewing her thumbnail. "I mean, whoever left the note must know what happened. Maybe they're too scared to show their face. We have to find out who left it!"

"Piece of cake!" came a voice from the shadows.

The distorted voice bounced eerily off the mine walls, startling Grace. She whirled around to see who had spoken.

Fred stepped in front of her, his hands balled tightly into fists, ready to deal with the intruder.

"We'll hack into the school security cameras," continued the mystery guest, stepping from the shadows into the lantern's circle of light.

"Oh, it's *you*!" Grace relaxed and dropped back to her seat. "I thought you couldn't come 'til later?"

"Jeeter, we're going to have to put a bell on you or something," Mai giggled, smiling up at him.

Fred stared at Mai's upturned face. His hands were still clenched into fists. "*You* know how to get into the school security cameras?" he asked.

"Geez, Fred," Grace said. "Chill! I told you before—Jeeter's a *genius* with computers."

Fred shot her a skeptical look as he turned around and stomped over to the brook, his curly black hair bouncing with every step. He reached down into the icy water and pulled out two dripping pop cans.

"Genius, yeah right," he mumbled, banging the cans down on the table. He yanked the tab off the first can and it emitted a loud warning hiss. As if in slow motion, a purple geyser exploded from the can and shot up into the air. It seemed to hover for a second before crashing down, covering Fred from head to toe in soda. Purple rivers ran down his face. Wordlessly, he handed the dripping can to Mai.

"Uh...thanks, Freddo," she said, taking a sip. "Mmm, grape. My favourite." She wrinkled her nose as sticky pop trickled from the side of the can onto her hand.

Fred's scowl deepened.

"Jeeter, what was that you said about the cameras?" Grace asked.

"It's no problem. I should be able to hack in on my dad's computer at home."

"*Hack in?*" Fred said. "Maybe I'm not a *genius*, but I know computers, too. It's not easy to hack into stuff."

"It might work," Grace said.

Mai slipped Fred a wet wipe from her backpack. "Thanks," he said, finally showing a hint of a smile as he mopped his face.

"I'll get right on it," Jeeter said. "Give me an hour, and then come over to my place, okay?"

"We'll come with you," Grace said. But she was talking to air. Jeeter was already gone.

"What's his hurry?" Fred asked. "You know, Grace, I don't think it was a good idea, letting him into our group." Soda-soaked curls hung in his blue eyes and he brushed them away. "I mean, we don't even really know the guy."

"Don't be paranoid," Grace replied. "He just moved here and he doesn't really know anyone. I told you. His mom died last year. Give him a chance."

"Fine," Fred mumbled. "I feel bad for him about his mom and all, but there's just something weird about that guy..."

* * *

Jeeter was standing on his front step when they arrived. "It worked!" he exclaimed as Grace, Fred, and Mai walked up the drive. "I told you it'd be a piece of cake!"

As she followed Jeeter inside, Grace noticed how tall he was. With his muscles and brush cut, he looked more like an action figure than a teenager only one year older than she was.

There were boxes stacked in Jeeter's living room, covering the couch and coffee table as if it was still moving day. But the basement was a different story. It was lit up with blinking lights and glowing screens from several computers. One of them caught her eye—it showed a map of mine sites around Cape Breton. She'd seen paper ones just like it in her dad's office.

"Where does your dad work, anyway?" Fred asked, echoing Grace's thoughts. "He lets you use all this?"

"Roger's never around. I do what I want."

"You call your dad by his first name?" Fred said. "That's weird."

"You want weird, look in the mirror."

"Knock it off, you guys," Grace said. "Hey, there's my locker!" She pointed to an image on one of the screens.

"How did you hack into the cameras?" Mai asked.

"It wasn't hard. Here, I'll start the feed over at the beginning." Jeeter sat at the terminal and pounded on the keys.

The picture was dark and grainy. First there was nothing but an empty hallway. The hall was usually filled with students laughing and banging locker doors. Grace never knew there was a camera watching everything they did. It was kind of creepy.

She gasped as a person suddenly appeared on the screen, walking toward the lockers. He was dressed in jeans and a hoodie, with the hood pulled up over his head. He took something out of his pocket and slid it into Grace's locker. Then he backed up and the screen went blank.

"That's no good," Grace sighed in frustration. "You can't even see his face."

"Let's watch it again," Jeeter said. "Maybe we missed something."

Jeeter started the video from the beginning. Grace, Mai, and Fred leaned in close to get a better look.

"Hey, I think something fell out of his pocket!" Fred leaned forward and touched the computer screen. "Right there!"

"Fred!" Grace yelped. "Hands off! I can't see."

"Oops, sorry," he said, hastily removing his hand. A purple fingerprint was smeared across the monitor.

Mai grabbed another wipe from her pack and tackled the purple trail. "There it is. Zoom in."

"The other side!" Fred said, as nothing but magnified floor tile came into view. He reached over to touch the keypad. "Here, let me—"

"Back off, *Freddo*." Jeeter elbowed him away. "I got it."

Suddenly, a crumpled envelope came into view. Only the first two lines of the address were visible:

"It can't be," Grace whispered.

"What's wrong?" asked Jeeter.

Fred and Mai looked at each other, eyes wide. Both spoke at the same time.

"This is going to be trouble!"

Chapter 3

"GRACE, IT'S 9:30," MAI SAID. "EARTH TO GRACE—CURFEW?"

Curfew. "Crap, I gotta go!" Grace grabbed her backpack and ran for the stairs. "I'll keep my walkie-talkie on. Call me later!" she called over her shoulder.

Grace raced through the streets. She used every shortcut she knew and flew into the driveway in record time. The windows of the hundred-year-old house her parents had inherited from her grandmother were still dark and the driveway was empty.

Phew! That was close, she thought. Dumping her pack inside the back door, she flicked on the light. The kitchen wasn't empty.

Her mother sat at the island, her hands wrapped around a steaming mug. The smell of fresh ground beans filled the air. *Uh-oh.* Her mother never drank coffee past five o'clock. And sitting in the dark? Well, that couldn't be a good sign.

"*Grace Elizabeth*, there you are," her mother said, granite eyes freezing Grace on the spot.

Both names—double uh-oh. This was worse than she thought. "Sorry I'm late. I had a flat tire and—"

"So," her mother interrupted. Her red manicured nails were tapping rapidly against her mug. "All ready for the math test tomorrow?"

"Math test? Umm...yeah," Grace said. She'd almost forgotten her alibi. "We got through all the review questions and—"

"Stop before you dig yourself any deeper!" Her mother banged her mug on the counter and coffee sloshed over the rim. "Jessica called looking for you. You remember Jessica, your study partner?" She waved Grace's note in the air. "Where were you, *really*?"

"Mom, it's not what you think."

"And what am I thinking?" She glanced at the discarded backpack by the door. "You'd better not have been traipsing around in those sinkholes again! They're dangerous. I thought we were past the daredevil behaviour... and the lying."

"Mom, I'm sorry. We weren't doing anything wrong, I swear.... We were just—" Grace looked at her mom's pinched face and was surprised to see a glint of grey hair at her temples. She looked older all of a sudden.

"You were just what?"

Grace couldn't quite swallow. Her throat felt like there was a boulder in it. She couldn't tell her mom about the note, not yet.

"You've always been adventurous, like your father." Her mother sighed and ran a hand through her shoulder-length hair. "I never really agreed with him taking you hunting for those bloody fossils, crawling over cliffs and digging in caves—ever since you could walk, practically." She sighed again. "I should have insisted that you stayed in ballet...but you were such a tomboy."

"I hated ballet," Grace whispered, "and the pink tights. All those girls with the same perfect hair and perfect nails." Grace pressed her lips together and looked down at her stubby fingers and chewed-off nails. It was the same old argument.

Her mother was staring at her own manicured fingertips. "Forget the ballet. I'm sorry I mentioned it." She grabbed a cloth and started viciously wiping up the spilled coffee. "You were so much more reckless after your father.... But your sessions with Dr. Solomon were helping. I thought things were getting better."

They stood staring at each other, her mother's last words hanging between them. Grace opened her mouth to speak and then closed it again. Her mother wouldn't care that this time was different. She'd just have to prove it.

"Go to bed, Grace," her mother said, finally breaking the silence. "We'll talk about it in the morning."

Grace trudged upstairs, dragging her pack behind her. She flopped onto the bed and stared at the ceiling, where a collage of star charts looked like a window up to the universe. It didn't have its normal calming effect. Restless, her eyes wandered around her room, finally stopping on the collection of fossil books her dad had bought her.

Memories of the fossil-hunting trips she and her dad had taken all over Nova Scotia—to places like Parrsboro, Joggins, and Blue Beach—flashed like a slide show in her head. Scaling cliffs, wading through river currents, and hiking over rough terrain.... *No! Stop it!* She forced herself to look away and the images faded from her mind. She was getting good at this.

Repression. Her therapist, Dr. Solomon, loved the word. He'd say it slowly, letting it roll off his tongue. Sometimes he'd add a chin stroke for good measure. He always looked pleased when he did this, like he'd discovered the Caramilk secret or something.

Grace tried to focus her whirling brain and sort out all the facts spinning around inside her head. Her dad had said he was going to check out some new sites around Point Aconi the day he disappeared, March fifth. Because the winter had been so mild, with hardly any snow, he had been able to keep doing his fieldwork right through the winter.

Point Aconi was about a fifteen-minute drive from Sydney Mines. The coal seam and fossil cliffs there were at the very tip of the point, beneath the lighthouse. The area was riddled with bootleg coal mines. No one lived there now, not since a gigantic sinkhole had swallowed most of the road five years ago. The government had re-located everyone who lived there and that's when a company had first tried to lease the land for strip mining. Her dad had always hoped the government would ban the mining and have Point Aconi declared a heritage site because of the wealth of fossils there.

But her dad's strip mining protests hadn't seemed to work. The strip mining deals, including the one for Point Aconi, had looked like they were going to be approved. Grace's dad had said he'd have to move fast to collect as many fossils as he could from the area because they would be destroyed when the mining started.

Several new sinkholes had formed out at Point Aconi in the months before the accident, creating entry points into another bootleg mining tunnel system. Because the tunnels followed the coal seams, there were almost always exposed fossils to be found, either scattered on the ground or visible in the walls. But Grace's dad hadn't let her go fossil-hunting with him on Saturdays like she usually did. He'd said it was too dangerous with the wet weather—that the ground was less stable than ever.

He had shown her the area on her map, which was an exact copy of the one he used. She'd always updated hers just like he did, writing in new sinkholes and fossil sites as he'd found them.

Maybe something did happen out there that day, Grace thought to herself. But they had found his car crashed into the ocean far away from Point Aconi. And someone at the fossil museum had said he'd returned to the office after he'd visited Point Aconi that day.

But now with the note, new doubts bloomed inside her. *What if Rick Stanley is involved?* Grace wondered. Maybe he had been the one that said her dad had returned to the museum. He could have been lying to cover his tracks.

The steps creaked as Grace's mother climbed the stairs. Grace waited for the familiar sound of the television. On many nights since the accident, Grace had woken up and heard it blaring. On these nights, she'd tiptoe into her parents' room and find her mom asleep, clutching her dad's picture. She'd stand there, watching her mother's tear-stained face as she slept and wondering what she was dreaming about.

Eventually, she'd shut off the television and tiptoe out. It was pretty much a ritual between them now, one they never discussed—like everything else.

Curious when she didn't hear the television, Grace padded down the hardwood floor of the hall in her sock feet. Light spilled from the open bedroom doorway. Her mother sat on the bed, facing away from her.

"Mom, what are you doing?"

"Why on earth are you still up?" her mother replied, hastily wiping fresh tears from her cheeks. She stuffed something in a box and put it on the top shelf of the closet.

"What's that?"

Grace's mother met her eyes briefly. "Just some old bills," she said. She turned on the television and climbed into bed. The blue light flickered eerily on her expressionless face. "You should be asleep."

She didn't look at Grace again.

Repression. There's that word again, Grace thought. Her mother was getting as good at it as she was. Maybe *she* should go see Dr. Solomon.

Returning to her room, Grace crawled under her covers, craving the escape of sleep.

KCHHHH! There was a familiar crackle from her backpack.

"Grace, come in," Fred's whispered voice sounded through the radio. "Are you there?"

Grace grabbed her walkie-talkie. "I'm here," she said. The walkie-talkies she and her friends had bought to communicate while exploring underground were also good for secret chats.

"What's the damage?" Mai chimed in.

"She was really ticked. 'We'll talk in the morning,' she said. That gives her more time to think up a punishment."

"Well, if she grounds you she can't watch you all the time," Fred said. "She works late."

"You're forgetting her spy next door, Snoopy Stuckless," Grace said. "But don't worry. I have a plan."

Chapter

4

GRACE STARED AT HER CLOCK. IT WAS ONE-THIRTY IN THE MORN-
ing. Endless questions were spinning around in her
head—questions with no answers.

Finally, she couldn't take it any longer. She had to
talk to someone. It was way too late to call Mai or Fred—
they'd be asleep for sure.

"Jeeter?" Grace whispered into her walkie-talkie. "Are
you awake?" She waited.

A few weeks ago, she and Jeeter had started chatting on
their walkie-talkies late at night when she couldn't sleep.
He always answered her call, no matter how late it was.

"I'm here," his voice echoed back. "Trouble sleeping again?"

"Yeah."

"Another bad dream?"

"Uh-huh," she sniffed, unexpected tears flooding her
eyes. "My dad was calling for me, but I couldn't find him."
She couldn't believe she'd said it. She'd never told anyone
what she saw in her dreams. But Jeeter understood. He'd
told her before that he had bad dreams, too, since his
mom had died.

"It's all right, Grace," he said. "No luck with the wave machine?"

"It's not helping."

"Okay. Tell me one of your stories, then. What about that trip you and your dad took to Parrsboro? You know, when he got that nickname, *Old Fossil.*"

"Again?" She smiled through her tears. The story was one of her favourites, too.

"It's a funny story."

"Okay." Grace sighed and closed her eyes, snuggling back into her pillow. She recounted the days when she and her dad had gone on amazing adventures under sunny skies...and finally drifted off to sleep.

"Now Grace, remember what I told you. Stay as far away from the cliff as it is high," her dad said.

Grace looked up at the towering cliff above them. "Why?"

"So if there is an avalanche or any rocks fall, you won't be under them."

Grace grinned. "Good tip, Dad. But all the fossils are over there!" She pointed to a pile of broken shale in a carved-out piece of the cliff face.

"Yes, that tends to be a problem," he said. "Let me worry about that, okay?" He smiled, ruffling her hair.

They were on a fossil tour in Parrsboro. Several tourists were in the group. Grace watched a tall lady trying to walk along the rocky shore in flip-flops. Two small kids were poking sticks at a dead jellyfish. These tourists weren't real fossil hunters, not like Grace and her dad.

"Excuse me," an older lady with a British accent said as she approached them.

"Good afternoon," Grace's dad said.

"You're the spitting image of my granddaughter, Lily," she said, beaming at Grace. "I just had to come over and say hello. Are you having a nice time with your grandfather?"

Grace's mouth fell open. Grandfather?

The lady turned to Grace's dad. "I would have loved to have my grandchildren with me, as well, but they're back in England."

"He's not my grandfather. He's my dad!" Grace said, giggling.

The lady's eyes widened. She stared at Grace's dad's grey beard and hair. "Oh, pardon me!" she said, her cheeks red.

"Understandable mistake," Grace's dad said. "I think of myself as an old fossil most of the time."

The lady apologized again and hurried off, obviously embarrassed.

"My word, that was funny!" Grace's dad exploded, doubling over with laughter. "Your mom would get a kick out of that, wouldn't she?"

Grace held her aching ribs and nodded.

Her dad started hobbling around, pretending he couldn't walk properly. "Give an old fellow a hand would you, young miss?" he asked in his best old-man voice.

"Give it up, Dad!"

"My word! I've got an ache in my back! I think my knee is giving out!"

They laughed hysterically the rest of the day.

That night they stayed at the Fundy Geological Museum as part of an overnight program. As they nestled in their sleeping bags, surrounded by dinosaurs, her dad whispered to her. "I'm so grateful we share this, Grace—this love of fossils. You don't know how much it means to me."

Grace heard the emotion in his voice and felt a lump in her throat. "Me too, Dad," she whispered back. "I love you."

Grace opened her eyes. She could swear she'd heard a cry. It must have wakened her. She lay there, listening for sounds in the deep quiet of the night. But it was dead silent. It must have been her own cry, she realized. She could still hear it, echoing in her head from her dream.

"I really miss you, Dad," she murmured into the dark.

Chapter
5

GRACE STARED DOWN AT HER BOWL OF SUGAR-OS, WAITING FOR the verdict. Her mother had sighed five times, glared three times, and was sure to speak at any moment.

"Grace—"

Here it comes, Grace thought. "Umm, Mom, what happened to the car?" she asked, trying to delay the inevitable. "It wasn't in the driveway last night."

"The car? Oh, it broke down on me while I was coming home from work. I just had that thing in for servicing last week!" she said, looking puzzled. "Rick Stanley was kind enough to give me a lift home. Lucky for me he happened to be driving by. Anyway, he was asking how we're doing. I invited him over for dinner."

"Why do you want him over here?"

"Rick's been a friend of your father's since they were children. He's been calling and wanting to come over and check on us for ages, but I just haven't been up to it. He has such wonderful stories about your father." She sighed and stared off into space.

"Mom?"

"Hmm? Oh, right, we were talking about you." Her mother poured a cup of coffee from the steaming carafe. "I thought about this all night, Grace. I'm going give you one more day of freedom, if you promise to behave. But starting tomorrow you're to come straight home after school. No detours and no going out."

Grace sat still, stunned. *No going out? Did she say no going out?*

"This is for your own good," her mother continued, wrapping her hands around the *Old Fossil* mug that Grace had made for her father. "I can't be worrying about you all the time, out doing goodness knows what, especially now that I have more night shifts at the ferry terminal...not to mention my manicure customers."

"Mom, no way!" Grace's spoon splattered into her cereal bowl. "I've got important stuff to do! It's not fair!"

"Fair? You think this is a debate? And what important stuff are you talking about? You're only thirteen, for heaven's sake." Her mother started to walk away, then turned back. Her face was grave. "I'm warning you, Grace," she said, tapping a brochure on the fridge as she left.

*   *   *

Grace was furious as she biked to school. Her mother was one extreme or the other lately. Grace never knew what she'd face. Sometimes her mom would get really upset and overreact as if she were some kind of army sergeant, like now. Other times, she'd be the total opposite, all gushy and gooey. Grace usually hated the gushy-gooey mood more; it felt fake. But it would have been better this morning—gushy-gooey mom would do anything she wanted.

"What are you going to do, Grace?" Mai typed away on the keyboard as they huddled around the computer monitor in class. They were supposed to be researching the tar ponds cleanup for a school project.

"I don't know. I'm grounded starting tomorrow. I wish we could go to Point Aconi today after school. But it would take too long to get there and my mom's not working tonight."

"But if you're not home tomorrow after school, you're gonna be toast," Fred piped in. "We'd be gone until dark."

"I've got to find out what's going on," Grace whispered. "I mean, think about it. The fossil museum is where Dad worked, and its name just happens to be on the envelope that some mystery guy left by my locker. Rick Stanley still works there. I never liked him all that much—my dad was always loaning him money." She wrinkled her nose at the memory. "My mom doesn't know about that, though. She thinks he's *nice*."

"Shhhh," Mai hushed. "Here comes Mr. Grange."

"And have we learned anything about the tar ponds and the cleanup project?" Mr. Grange asked. "Or are you three too busy chatting?"

"No, Mr. Grange," Mai said. "We were working on it."

"What have you got so far?" Mr. Grange asked.

Grace gulped. She hadn't been paying any attention to the sites Mai had looked up.

"The steel plant in Sydney left behind over one million tons of contaminated soil," Mai recited. "The pollutants have run off into Sydney Harbour and caused fish contamination and many other environmental problems."

Mr. Grange nodded. "Go on," he prodded.

"It's one of the biggest contaminated sites in North America," Mai continued. "There have been a lot of attempts to do something about the mess in the past, but nothing has worked so far. The government is hoping a new cleanup program will work."

Mr. Grange seemed satisfied. "Very good," he said approvingly. "Carry on."

"Nice going, Mai," Grace said after Mr. Grange had circled the room and returned to the front of the class.

"Thanks," Mai grinned. "Now what were you saying again?"

"Get this—" Grace lowered her voice and jumped back into their previous conversation. "My mom's car broke down the other night and Stanley just *happened* to be there. He drove her home. Now he's coming to dinner! I mean, what's he after?"

"Rick Stanley? So does this mean we're going to the fossil museum?" Fred asked. "Grace, are you nuts? Don't you remember when you broke in there and tried to steal back all the fossils your dad donated? You knocked over that big display case. Your picture is probably plastered on their wall with a sign above it that says *Most Wanted!*"

"Fred's right," Mai said. "For once. Besides, your mom will totally freak if she finds out what you're up to."

"What do you mean, for once?" Fred huffed. "Seriously, Grace. You said your mom was acting really weird lately. She could totally blow it and send you to one of the prison camps for kids. I saw it on the Discovery Channel—*Problem Kids: Last Resort*. It's not pretty!"

Fred didn't know how close he was about the prison camp for kids. Grace's mom had actually threatened to send her to one when she'd broken into the museum. Her mom had even brought home the brochure. It was covered in pictures of kids smiling and wearing identical clothes, hiking up Cape Smokey.

It was the same brochure that Grace's mom had pointed to on the fridge that morning. Even though she'd never actually *said* she'd send Grace there, it was obvious that's what she meant—another of her mom's extremes.

"You'll come back programmed like some robot, dressed in a uniform and eating tuna sandwiches!" Fred stood up and jerked his arms up and down in a lame robot imitation. "And you'll talk weird, like 'Hello, my name is Grace Elizabeth. Hello, my name is Grace Elizabeth!'"

Grace looked down at her tie-dyed T-shirt and ripped jeans. *Uniform? No way.*

"Tuna? What's wrong with tuna?" Mai asked. "It's full of omega-3. You know—brain food." She clutched her lunch bag. "You could use some brain food, Freddo, that's for sure!"

"Whatever," Fred said, rolling his eyes. "Anyways, Grace, you can't go to the fossil museum. You'll be arrested."

"Everyone's probably forgotten about that," Grace said. "And it was all that security guard's fault anyway. *He* tried to tackle *me*. I ducked and he's the one who fell into the display case. Besides, we're not going there."

"Where else is there?" Mai looked confused.

"Point Aconi. I'm sure Dad was fossil-hunting out there that day. I mean, no one even checked the area because someone at the fossil museum said he went back to the office that afternoon. But what if it was Stanley that said that, to cover his tracks? Maybe there's a clue out there somewhere..."

The bell rang. Grace was glad of the distraction. Chairs scraped and the sound level jumped to a roar as chattering students herded toward the door.

Fred stood up and slung his backpack over his shoulder. "I'm busy at lunch. I'll catch up with you guys later."

"You're the one who's always Mr. Spy Guy," Mai said. "What's more important than this?"

"I have to check something out. I'll tell ya later."

"Fred's up to something," Mai muttered to Grace as they watched him walk away.

*   *   *

Grace and Mai met up with Jeeter in the cafeteria at lunch. Mai bought an egg sandwich. Grace noticed that

Mai's lunch bag was missing and smiled to herself. It was probably ditched in her locker with an uneaten tuna sandwich still inside.

They snagged a vacant picnic table on the edge of the football field, far away from any unwelcome ears. "I think I've figured out how to get away for a while after school tomorrow," Grace said, peeling a slice of pepperoni off her pizza and popping it into her mouth. "Jessica owes me big. She blew my cover last night about studying together."

Jeeter gobbled down a handful of fries. "What's Swim Star gonna do?"

"I'll get her to pretend to be me and go to my place after school. It works out perfectly 'cause we're off tomorrow afternoon for that teachers' meeting. Plus, my mom's working."

"But what if your mom calls? I mean, Jessica could be your twin, but she doesn't sound anything like you." Mai unwrapped her sandwich and took an unenthusiastic bite. "Besides, it takes *forever* to bike all the way out to Point Aconi. Can't we go on the weekend?"

"I can't," Grace replied. "I'm grounded and my mom will be home. I'll just tell Jessica not to answer the phone. Then Mom will check in with Stuckless instead. He'll tell her I'm home and *voila*—it's perfect!" She grinned. "What could go wrong?"

Chapter
6

IT TOOK LOTS OF ARM-TWISTING, BUT JESSICA FINALLY AGREED to miss her swim team practice the next day and cover for Grace.

"Only one problem," Jessica said. "You said this Stuckless guy is pretty sharp, right?"

"That's for sure. He's King of the Snoops," Grace replied.

"Well, I'm gonna need it then," Jessica said, holding out her hand. "You're gonna have to give me the hat or you'll be busted for sure."

Grace reluctantly slipped off her hat. Her fingers brushed the embroidered letters as Jessica tugged it from her hand. A hollow feeling filled her, like she'd just given away part of herself.

❋   ❋   ❋

Hours later at Black Hole, Grace ran her fingers through her hair for the millionth time. She felt weird without her lucky cap. It was like her brain wouldn't work properly or something.

"Grace?" Fred said, waving a hand in front of her face. "Come back down and join us earthlings."

"Sorry," she said, "what were you saying?"

"Nothing important—just how we're *not* going to get arrested or killed!"

"Chill, Freddo. It'll be a piece of cake," Jeeter said.

"Sure, Mr. Piece of Cake. Why don't you just hack into the fossil museum computers and *all will be revealed*!" Fred waved his hands in front of Jeeter's face like a magician. "It shouldn't be any problem for a *genius* like you."

"What's that supposed to mean?"

"Well, you're such a wizard with *Roger*'s computer. You could probably solve the whole mystery."

"Knock it off, Fred." Mai poked him in the ribs. "Just ignore him," she told Jeeter with a smile. "His brain has turned to chocolate mush from all the candy bars he eats!"

"No one's getting arrested," Grace said. "I told you; we're not going to the fossil museum. We're going out to Point Aconi. If Rick Stanley did lie about seeing my dad, then maybe something happened out there. We'll have to be careful, though. There's probably a lot more sinkholes. My dad said the area was more dangerous when it rained, and it's been raining buckets lately."

"Great," Fred gulped. "Killer sinkholes!"

Grace unfolded her map on the wooden table. "We'll have to hike through the woods here." She traced a line with her finger on the map. "The woods are really thick, but they'll give us more cover and they're farther away from the strip mine site."

"Wouldn't it be easier to go in by the mine site?" Jeeter asked. "All the trees would be cleared."

Grace shook her head. "We can't. They have tons of security guards roaming around because of all the protests and vandalism. And they aren't friendly."

"Oh, yeah." Fred jumped up and started to pace. "Didn't you tell us a guy got punched in the face by some security goon at a protest?"

"I remember that," Mai gasped.

Fred's foot was tapping a mile a minute. "Maybe we should forget about Point Aconi. At least the fossil museum doesn't have killer sinkholes!" He lowered his voice as if he was telling a ghost story. "Besides, didn't someone die when they fell into a sinkhole up there last year?"

"That was in Glace Bay!" Grace replied.

Grace turned to Mai for support. But Mai was nervously peeling small splinters of wood from the tabletop with her fingernail. Grace felt a sinking feeling in her stomach. *What if they don't go?* she thought to herself. They couldn't chicken out on her now. She wouldn't be able to do this alone.

"So, are we going to help Grace or not?" Jeeter challenged, staring at Fred and Mai. "Aren't you supposed to be the *fossil hunters*? Not scared of a little hike, are you?"

Fred looked insulted. "Of course we'll help. We're always here for Grace. Aren't we, Mai?"

Mai let out a nervous giggle.

It did the trick and the ominous mood seemed to vanish.

"Great, then it's settled!" Grace said.

Fred, Mai, and Jeeter nodded in approval.

"Since it's still early and it's my last official day of freedom..." Grace started with a smile, "why don't we check out the tunnel by the Halfway Road pit?"

"Seriously?" Fred said. "Awesome! We haven't been through the tunnels for months. Let's go!" He clicked on his flashlight and hurried past the brook into the tunnel. Within seconds, his light had disappeared into the blackness.

"Where's he going?" Jeeter asked.

"One of the bootleg tunnels running from here ends at an old open pit mine at Halfway Road," Mai said. "Great fossils."

"Wouldn't it be easier to bike there?" He pointed up toward ground level. "You know, like normal people? It would definitely be faster!"

"What's the fun in that?" Grace laughed.

"Come with me. I'll show you." Mai grabbed Jeeter's hand and tugged him along.

Jeeter looked back at Grace. *Save me!* he mouthed.

Grace waved him on with a smirk. Jeeter didn't seem too happy to be alone with Mai. They disappeared into the dark, their bobbing flashlights fading quickly. Grace took her time before following behind them, enjoying the quiet.

The dark tunnels didn't scare her at all. She'd gotten used to them from fossil-hunting with her dad. "I sure wish you were with me now, Dad," she whispered into the blackness.

"Grace, come in," Mai's tinny voice called out from her walkie-talkie.

"What's up?" Grace answered.

"Where are you?"

"Close. I'll be there in a sec." Grace picked up her pace, careful to watch her footing on the slick tunnel floor. Water drip-dripped a constant beat along with her footsteps as she turned right then left down different arms of the warren of tunnels.

Grace bent low through a narrow section under Main Street. Since the tunnels were all hand-dug, they shrunk and expanded with no set pattern and she had to pay careful attention not to trip or bonk her head. Fred had smacked his head more than once when racing through the them.

She rounded another sharp turn and, instead of the expected blue sky from the opening at the pit, she faced glaring flashlights.

"Did we take a wrong turn?" she asked, swinging her beam back the way she'd come.

"Nope," Fred said.

"Then where's the opening?"

"Gone," Mai said softly.

"Gone?" Grace echoed.

"Cave-in!" The glow from Fred's flashlight made ghoulish shadows on his face.

Grace ran her light up and down the wall of earth and rock where the entrance to the pit opening once stood. "I wonder when this happened..." she mused aloud.

"We haven't been here for ages," Mai said. "It could have been anytime."

"Good thing we weren't here when it happened," Fred added. "We'd be pancakes...dead ones!"

"No kidding," Jeeter said. "Interesting hobby you guys have."

Grace knelt down. Her flashlight picked up distinctive shadows on the flat rocks. "Hey, look at this."

"What?" Mai bent low beside her.

"Stigmaria fossil." Grace held up a large piece of slate in her gloved hand.

"That's a great one," Mai said. "Look at the ridging on the root, there." She ran the tip of her finger along the dark ridges.

"What is that, a *plant*?" Jeeter didn't sound impressed. "Where are the raptor bones?"

"Hey, Jeeto, a little respect," Fred said. "These *plants* are a lot older than your raptors—by, like, over two hundred million years."

"Okay, fine," Jeeter mocked. "They're *really old* plants. But I don't see them starring in a movie!"

"Ya know, you're a bit of a—"

BAARRROOOMMM!!!

Suddenly, the ground rumbled. Bits of rock and grass rained down from above them.

"Ouch!" Fred yelped, rubbing his head.

"What's going on?" Mai cried.

Larger rocks started tumbling from the ceiling and walls. Grace scrambled to her feet. A table-sized piece of slate thundered down to the ground and shattered beside her.

"We've got to get out of here!" Jeeter shouted.

"Run!" Mai screamed.

Chapter 7

MAI TOOK OFF DOWN THE TUNNEL.

"That's not the way back to Black Hole!" Fred yelled to her. He raced after Mai as she flew around the corner.

"Fred, wait!" Grace called out, imagining him running into a wall, or worse. She and Jeeter followed behind him. But he disappeared around another turn before they could catch up.

"Are we going in a circle?" Jeeter called back to Grace after they took another right turn.

"Seems like it!"

They veered to the right yet again. This time, they were greeted by a beam of sunlight at an opening. There was no sign of Fred and Mai. Cautiously, they stepped out into a thick cluster of trees.

"Over here," Mai whispered from a few metres away.

Grace and Jeeter crawled over to where Mai and Fred were hiding.

"Look!" Mai pulled back some branches. They were on the opposite side of the old Halfway Road pit, but it wasn't the same quiet spot they were used to. "I think that's what caused the falling rocks in the tunnel," she said, pointing to a bunch of bulldozers and backhoes buzzing around fresh piles of dirt and rock.

"What are they doing here?" Fred asked.

Grim realization washed over Grace. "The government must have issued a lease to the mining company after all," she said glumly.

"What do you mean?" Jeeter asked.

"This was one of my dad's projects with the anti-strip-mining group. I even protested with him. He thought this site was a win for sure because it's right in town!" Grace stepped through the trees. Fred, Mai, and Jeeter followed behind her.

"Sorry, Grace," Jeeter murmured. He squeezed her shoulder.

"Thanks." Grace could feel tears stinging her eyes. All of her dad's hard work was going down the drain. There hadn't been any more protests since he'd disappeared.

Grace and the others watched the hornet's nest of activity down in the pit. The name Breton Hauling Limited and the initials BHL were all over the equipment. That wasn't the name of any mining company Grace remembered. This one must be new.

"We should leave, Grace," Fred said. "We could get into trouble for trespassing if we get caught here."

"Yeah, I guess," Grace replied.

Suddenly, a pickup truck sped into the pit, pulling in beside another one parked close to where they were standing. Grace recognized the truck, even before its driver got out. The truck's owner spied them and strode briskly toward them.

"Hello, Grace."

Grace stared at her next-door neighbour, Mr. Stuckless, but didn't answer him. Mai poked her in the ribs.

"You kids can't be here. It's private property."

"We're not doing anything," Grace finally replied.

"Well, it's a working pit now. You have to leave, for your own safety."

Grace folded her arms across her chest and scowled.

"Not planning a protest, now, are you?" Stuckless demanded.

"Maybe," Grace snapped. "You're not allowed here!"

Mr. Stuckless's smile disappeared. "Not a good joke. But we have a lease now anyway, so we most definitely are allowed here." He pointed toward the street. "But the same can't be said for you kids. You're trespassing!"

Grace felt a hand tugging on her sleeve. "C'mon," Mai murmured. "Let's go!"

Without saying another word, Grace turned and strode back through the trees. Mai, Fred, and Jeeter followed behind her. Silently, they walked back to Black Hole to get their bikes.

"I wonder when they reopened the pit," Fred said, hopping on his bike.

"I never heard a thing about it," Grace said. "But then it was my dad that filled me in on all that stuff." She tugged viciously on one of her pack straps. "Mom doesn't care about it!"

No one said anything.

They rode wordlessly back up Pitt Street and with a wave split off into different directions. Grace pedalled slowly toward home. Her mom's car was in the driveway, with a shiny red sports car behind it. *Oh, great!* she thought to herself. She didn't feel much like company.

Grace opened the back door and was instantly surrounded by a swirl of delicious smells. *Mom's cooking?* she thought as she walked toward the stove. *She never cooks. Mmmm...smells like boiled dinner.* Grace lifted the lid to peer inside. She grabbed a fork and snagged a piece of corned beef. *Delicious!* Her stomach rumbled.

"Sweetie, is that you?" came her mom's voice. "We're in the living room."

Uh-oh. Gushy-gooey mom front and centre. The mystery guest was probably some manicure client—a ballerina mom, with her luck. Grace looked down at her clothes—only a bit dirty. She kicked off her muddy shoes and grabbed a handful of grapes from the fruit bowl on the counter.

As she walked through the dining room, Grace noticed that the table was set for three—with the good china. Reluctantly, she continued into the living room.

"Surprise, honey," her mom smiled. "We have a dinner guest."

Grace almost choked on the grape in her mouth. There he was, right in front of her face, sitting in her dad's chair, talking to her mom! She curled her left hand into a fist, squishing the grapes in her palm. Juice oozed between her fingers.

"Hi there, Grace," Rick Stanley said from his seat in her dad's chair. His sympathetic gaze met hers. "I'm really sorry for your loss."

Grace stared at him, looking for some sign of what he was up to. What did he know? What had he done?

"That's sweet. Thank you, Rick," her mother said. "Grace thanks you, too. Don't you, Grace?"

Grace wondered what she had expected to happen when she ran into Rick Stanley. That she'd be able to tell what he'd done? That she would know what he was thinking? If only she could see inside his brain. Stanley shifted in his seat and it seemed to Grace that he was avoiding her gaze. Was he hiding something?

"Grace!" Her mother's voice slashed across the room like a whip.

"What?"

"Wash up for dinner."

Grace stormed out of the room. The nerve of Stanley, sitting in her dad's chair. She wanted to yank him out of there. And her mom was letting him! Grace dumped the grape pulp in the bathroom garbage and scrubbed her hands in scalding water. Glancing at her reflection, she noticed a streak of coal dust along her cheekbone. Had her mom seen it, too? Not that it mattered anyway—she was already grounded.

When Grace opened the bathroom door off the kitchen, her mom was pulling scones from the oven. Were those Nana's famous raisin scones?

"Where's Stanley?" Grace asked.

"Stanley? Since when do we call people by their last names? You weren't raised in a swamp!" Her mother banged the baking sheet down. The scones bounced on the counter, and one fell onto the floor. "Look what you made me do," she said, yanking off the oven mitts. "And I broke a nail!"

"Sorry, Mom," Grace mumbled. She scooped the hot biscuit up off the floor.

Her mom sighed. "I know this isn't easy," she said. "But this is the first company we've had since...." She broke off. "Please try to be civilized."

Grace felt a ripple of guilt. "Sorry," she repeated. "Can I help?"

"Why don't you grab the butter? Everything else is just about ready."

Grace opened the fridge and spotted fresh-cooked blueberry grunt on the shelf. Her heart sank. "Where did the blueberries for the grunt come from?" she asked. "Not the ones from the freezer?"

Her mother looked puzzled. "Yes, why? What's wrong?"

"Those were the ones Dad and I picked last August. Remember? We found this great blueberry patch in

Florence." Grace stared at the blueberry grunt. "I was saving them...for pancakes..."

"Well, I can make you pancakes anytime you want, and the grocery store has lots of..." Her mother stopped. "Oh, I see."

Grace stared at the dessert, wishing the berries back into the freezer. She couldn't believe they were going to end up in Rick Stanley's mouth.

"I'm sorry, sweetheart." Her mom patted her on the shoulder. "You and I will go out there and pick a pile of them in August."

Grace faked a smile and tried not to let her mom know that it wasn't the same thing. Not even close! It felt like no matter what she did or how tight she held on, her dad kept slipping away from her.

Chapter
8

"COME ON, LET'S TRY TO HAVE A NICE SUPPER," GRACE'S MOM COAXED, giving her a searching look. "I made your favourite..."

Grace let out a deep breath and nodded. Maybe she could turn this situation around and find out what Stanley was doing here. Remembering her nana's favourite saying, *you catch more flies with honey than vinegar*, she vowed to be on her best behaviour.

That lasted about thirty seconds—until the moment she saw Rick Stanley walking toward her dad's chair at the dining room table. *He's not getting that chair, too!* Grace thought to herself. Before she realized it, she'd slipped in behind him just as he was about to sit down.

"Sorry, my chair," Grace said.

Stanley jumped up, banging his knee against the table. "Whoa! I didn't see you."

Grace's mother shot her a withering stare. "*Your* chair?"

"It is now," Grace said.

"No problem," Stanley chortled. "There are lots of seats." He pulled the place setting from Grace's usual seat to the one beside her mother.

Grace's mom proceeded to load their plates with steaming heaps of corned beef, cabbage, potatoes, and carrots. Grace lathered butter on a scone and took a bite. It was nothing like her nana's—it was hard as a rock! Her mom's cooking was awful, the rare times she even tried it. Thank goodness boiled dinner was bad-cook-proof.

Crunching on the tough biscuit, Grace watched Rick Stanley as he ate. It was disappointing. He acted very normal and boring, not at all like a criminal. She felt like her chance to get answers out of him was slipping away. Suddenly, she remembered the expensive-looking sports car in the driveway. "I like your car," she blurted out.

Stanley beamed. "She's a beauty, isn't she? The only one on the island, the dealer told me."

"Wow!" Grace said. "You must have won the lotto or something."

Stanley chuckled. "I wish."

"All my dad ever had was an old pickup. I guess the fossil museum pays way better than it used to."

Grace's mom gasped into her wine glass. "Grace!"

Stanley's face went bright red. "No, that's okay. I, uh, just came into some money. A relative passed away..."

"Oh, I'm terribly sorry," Grace's mom said.

"It's all right. It was a...distant relative." He grabbed the serving bowl and scooped out a second helping of boiled dinner. "This is delicious, Pat. It's been a long time since I had good corned beef."

"My pleasure," Grace's mom said, sipping her wine. "It's nice to have company again."

For Grace, dinner seemed to go on forever. Stanley was asking her mom all kinds of questions about how she was feeling, what had she been doing, how things were going—blah, blah, blah. He didn't even flinch when he bit into one of the cement scones, not even a twitch! He was putting on the nice-guy act and she'd had enough.

"Who was it?"

Stanley stared blankly at Grace. "Who was what?"

"Your relative?"

"Oh. Ah, it was an aunt, a great aunt...on my father's side."

"What was her name?" Grace asked, putting on her sweetest smile. "Did she live around here?"

"*Grace.*" Her mom's voice was raised to the *watch it* level.

"No, no. That's okay." Stanley held Grace's gaze. "It was Great Aunt Beatrice. She lived in Baddeck." He patted his shirt pocket and stood up abruptly. "I think I left my cell in the car and I need to make a quick call. Excuse me, ladies? I'll be right back."

"Oh, of course," Grace's mom said.

Grace watched Stanley from under her lashes. She could have sworn he gave her a dirty look as he passed by, but it disappeared almost immediately. Was she imagining things?

Grace's mom frowned at her across the table. "What are you up to?"

"What did I do?"

"You know perfectly well!" she scolded. "What's all this third-degree business?"

"I was just making conversation."

"Hmm...well, we could do with a little less of that from here on in," she said. "I'll just finish up here and then we'll get the tea on for dessert as soon as Rick gets back."

Grace broke up pieces of her uneaten biscuit with her fork.

"A bit tough, weren't they?"

"Just a little," Grace said. *More like frozen hockey pucks!*

Her mom shrugged. "At least the corned beef was tender."

Grace nodded, deciding not to mention that the vegetables must have boiled forever—they were so waterlogged that they disintegrated as soon as she touched them with her fork.

Grace and her mom waited...and waited. It seemed like Stanley had been gone for ages. Grace wiggled impatiently in her chair. Who would he be talking to all this time? Men never talked on the phone longer than they had to. Not her dad, anyway. Jeeter either. She grabbed the empty serving dish on the table. "I'll get the dessert."

Grace walked through the swinging door into the kitchen and froze. Rick Stanley was standing by the open doorway of the basement. She couldn't tell if he was going down or coming back up.

"What are you doing?"

Stanley spun around. "Uh, looking for the bathroom."

"That's the basement! Bathroom's here." She jabbed her elbow at the open door to her left.

"My mistake," he murmured. He glanced down into the dark cavern of the basement. "Your light is out."

Grace's mom entered the kitchen as Stanley finished speaking, catching the end of what he had said. She rushed over to the open basement door and shut it. "We don't go down there...Jonathan's office is in the basement..." she trailed off.

"Oh." He nodded sympathetically. "That's right—I think you may have mentioned that when we talked before. I can fix that light, if you like."

"I, um...no, thank you," Grace's mom replied. "Not right now."

"You know," Stanley added, stroking his chin, "if you're putting off going down there because you don't know what to do with everything, I could help you sort it out."

"Go through his things?" Grace's mother looked shocked. "Oh, no, I couldn't."

"I understand," he said. "It's just that there could be fossils or documents that Jonathan may have wanted to go to the museum."

"Oh, I hadn't thought of that." Grace's mom leaned against the basement door.

"He sure loved the museum," Stanley added, his voice softer.

"Yes, he certainly did." Grace's mom's eyes glazed over. She wrapped her arms around herself, like she had a chill.

"Are you sure you don't want me to fix that light anyway?" he asked, reaching for the doorknob.

Grace's Spidey senses were tingling. Stanley seemed determined to get into the basement for some reason. "No!" she cried.

The exclamation startled Grace's mom out of her trance. "Thank you, Rick," she said firmly, "but we can do that another day, perhaps. There's no hurry, since we don't go down there."

"No problem." His hand lingered on the doorknob. "Call me when you're ready. I can help."

"I know I can't put it off forever. But I locked it after...." she trailed off. "For the life of me, I can't remember where I put the key. I'll have to find it first."

"Sure," Stanley said understandingly. "Just let me know if you need some help."

She nodded. "Now, who's ready for dessert?"

"Thanks, Pat," Stanley said, "but I couldn't eat another bite. Not after two helpings of dinner." He patted his stomach. "I should get going."

"Well, it was good of you to come by," Grace's mom replied. "We really appreciate your concern for us. You're always welcome here."

"I'll be sure to take you up on that." Stanley turned to Grace. "Take it easy, kid. Drop by the museum anytime."

Grace attempted a smile, but she was sure all she'd managed was a grimace—if her mom's frown was any indication. But she couldn't help it.

After Stanley left, Grace's mom made her help with the cleanup. Every second seemed like an hour. She had to tell Fred, Mai, and Jeeter about Stanley.

Finally in her room, Grace fumed at her dead walkie-talkie and slapped it into the charger. Her mom was now sitting by the phone in the living room, so she couldn't call anyone for a private conversation.

The fossil museum was her dad's creation and here Stanley was, acting like he owned it! Plus, he'd tried to sneak into her dad's office—hadn't he? Her mom would say her imagination was going wild. But why else would he want to go down into their grungy old basement? What was he after?

Chapter 9

MAI HELD UP HER WALKIE-TALKIE. "HAS EVERYONE GOT THEIR RA-dios charged up?"

Grace nodded, anxious to get going. She *had* to find something today—it might be her last chance to figure out what had really happened to her father. She'd basically interrogated her mom on the whereabouts of her dad's office key as they'd eaten their way through the blueberry grunt last night. But all she'd gotten was a stomach ache from the gluey blue muck.

Mai hadn't even been all that impressed with her Rick Stanley story. It had kind of lost something in translation when she'd whispered it over the bathroom stall in an extended washroom break. But Mai had at least agreed that the timing was pretty strange for him to show up all of a sudden.

"All charged," Fred chimed in. "I also replenished the choco stash. You know, just in case." He patted his back-pack.

"That's great, Fred." Mai shook her head. "I'm sure your chocolate cakes will come in handy when you're gushing blood from some cut you got tripping over a rock."

Jeeter held up his walkie-talkie. "These things are from the stone ages. How come you guys don't use cell phones? I already had one of those."

"The walkie-talkies work down in the tunnels," Mai said, pointing at the ground. "No cell phone towers down there."

Jeeter grunted and got on his bike. Grace, Mai, and Fred followed his lead and the four of them started pedalling away from the school grounds.

They headed out of town, through Florence, and toward Point Aconi. As she sped down the quiet roads, Grace's mind was racing as fast as her bicycle, wondering what they might find out there. It seemed like she'd only blinked and they were on the winding Point Aconi Road.

They hid their bikes behind some trees at the barricade where the road had been closed due to the sinkhole. As they prepared to hike around the gaping crater, Grace automatically lifted her hands to adjust her hat, then let them fall again. She kept forgetting it was on someone else's head.

"This is a weird place for your dad to go alone, isn't it?" Jeeter stated. "Besides, wouldn't he have had trouble getting past security?"

"I hate to say it, but I agree with the Jeetman for once," Fred said, staring out beyond the barricade as he munched on a chocolate bar. "It *is* kinda weird. I mean, who goes out into woods with killer sinkholes everywhere?"

Leave it to Fred to be Mr. Drama, Grace thought. It *was* strange, though, she admitted to herself. She remembered it had been pouring rain the day of her dad's accident, which would have made it even more dangerous. What had been important enough to make her dad go against his own advice?

"Hey, Grace, what's the plan again?" Jeeter asked.

"We'll split into two teams so we can cover more ground," Grace replied. She switched on her walkie-talkie and tucked her knife into her pocket.

"Great," Mai said cheerily. She walked over to stand beside Jeeter. "You and Fred can be Team One and Jeeter and I will be Team Two."

Mai's batting eyelashes were getting a little annoying, Grace thought. "No, Jeeter and I will go through this break in the trees. It's closer to the strip mine and it'll be more dangerous. You and Fred can go through that opening over there," she said, pointing to a gap in the treeline a short distance away. "That way's safer."

Mai glared at Grace, her smile nowhere in sight. Was she going to say no?

"Sounds great to me," Fred said, shooting a smirk at Jeeter. "I like safer!"

"But you'll still have to watch out for security guards around any paths or clearings—there's probably a lot of them," Grace instructed. "Lock channel three on hands-free. That way we can hear one another if anything happens."

"Sure, Grace, whatever you say," Mai said flatly. "Like always." Without another word, she disappeared through the trees.

"Hey, wait up!" Fred called as he scrambled off to catch up with her. "Last one there is a rotten..." His voice faded as he disappeared into a sea of green.

This is getting crazy, Grace thought as she and Jeeter made their way into the dense woods. *Fred is jealous of Jeeter; Mai is jealous of me*. It was so not like that between her and Jeeter. He wasn't her boyfriend or anything. He just, well, really knew what she was going through, that's all.

The path was rockier than Grace had expected. The branches were so close together that it was like night under their treetop canopy—everything looked smudged.

She could barely see Jeeter when she looked behind her, and they were just a few metres apart.

The only sounds were Mai and Fred's heavy breathing echoing eerily over the airways. That, and the occasional grunt as Fred tripped over a root, or his own feet.

"Watch it, Fred!" Mai complained loudly. "You almost knocked me over again!"

"Sorry," Fred called back. "I didn't see you."

"Shhhh," Grace hissed into her walkie-talkie. "Do you guys want to get caught? That's it! Radio silence from now on—I'm switching off!" She flipped the power button on her walkie-talkie and it went silent.

"Man, you'd think they could hold it together for half an hour," Jeeter said. He turned his radio off, too.

"I know they're a bit hard to take sometimes." Grace vaulted over a fallen log, her feet crunching on dry twigs and leaves as she landed. "But they're still my best friends."

"I know." He kept pace beside her. "Did you come here much with Jona—I mean, your dad?"

She nodded, memories immediately crashing in around her at the mention of her dad. "This was my favourite place to come, when it was safe enough and he'd let me. He loved this place the best, so I did too."

"You're so lucky to have had a dad like him. How long did he work at the museum?"

"You really want me to talk about him?"

"I told you," Jeeter said, "I like hearing about your times together. It makes me feel like I was there, too. Roger and I don't do anything together. All he does is work."

"I spend so much time trying *not* to think about him, sometimes my head feels like it's going to explode," Grace sighed. "Mom just cries, so I can't talk to her. Dr. Solomon, well, he gets paid to talk to me. And Fred and Mai are great, but they don't understand. They've never lost anyone. Not like you."

Jeeter coughed. "Grace, I have to tell you—"

"Shhhh!" she silenced him suddenly. "Did you hear that?"

Grace looked off to the left. The trees had thinned out quite a bit, and she could see a gravel road with rock piles scattered around it. They must have wandered closer to the edge of the strip mine site than she had planned.

She was about to motion that they swing right, back into deeper cover, when an electronic squawk filled the air. Startled, Grace checked her walkie-talkie—it was still off. She turned and whispered to Jeeter, "Was that you?"

"No," he said in a low voice. "It was someone else."

Grace froze. Uneasiness curdled in the pit of her stomach.

"Who do you think—?" Jeeter began.

Grace shook her head, holding a finger to her lips. She crouched, pulling him down beside her. They peered through the trees toward the road. Someone was walking along the gravel.

The man turned his head left and right, like he was searching for something. Was he looking for them? Maybe they hadn't hidden their bikes well enough. Jeeter put his arm around Grace's shoulders and pulled her close to him. His strong arm reassured her—until she saw their stalker's face.

Stuckless!

Chapter
10

GRACE GASPED, THEN SLAPPED HER HAND OVER HER MOUTH. Stuckless stopped and peered into the trees toward them. Grace held her breath, hoping the gloomy forest hid them from view.

There was another squawk. "Dad, did you find them?" came a voice through the walkie-talkie.

"No," Stuckless replied. "We must have missed them." He turned abruptly and strode off.

Grace and Jeeter stayed there, still and silent as the woods, for several minutes.

"I think it's safe," Jeeter finally said, standing up. He grabbed Grace's hand and pulled her to her feet.

"That was close," Grace muttered.

"Yeah. I hope he doesn't catch your buddies."

"Crap!" Grace cried. "Our walkie-talkies are still off. We'd better find them." She switched her walkie-talkie back on and bolted off through the trees.

Almost immediately, the woods got thicker and her steps got slower. Was she even going in the right direction? How do you check your location on a map when you're surrounded by trees? Suddenly, Fred's voice crackled over her walkie-talkie.

"Hello?" he called.

Grace waited for Mai to answer. She didn't.

"Is anyone there?" he continued.

Fred's voice sounded weird. And where was Mai? It sounded like he was alone.

"Mai, is that you?" Fred's voice rose, sounding panicked.

Grace was just about to answer when—

"AAAAHHHH!"

Fred's frantic cry was followed by static.

"Fred?" Grace yelled into the walkie-talkie, her heart pounding in her chest. "Fred! Are you okay?"

No answer.

Grace's hand clenched her walkie-talkie. "Mai, are you with Fred?"

"No, he was behind me somewhere," Mai answered, sounding breathless. "Sorry, I was yelling, but you didn't seem to be able to hear me. I think my transmit button was stuck. I'm going back now to find him."

"Come on, Jeeter," Grace called behind her. "We've got to find Fred!"

Jeeter didn't answer.

Grace looked slowly over her shoulder. "Jeeter?"

She was alone.

Where did he go? Grace wondered. He'd been right behind her.

Grace hesitated, worried. Should she look for him? Maybe he was in trouble, too. But what about Fred? She stared off into the woods, willing Jeeter to appear. Everything was falling apart.

"Grace!" Mai shouted so loudly that the walkie-talkie shrieked. "I found him! He's not moving!"

Grace didn't have to think; she was already running.

Branches smacked her face and scratched her arms as she raced through the dense forest. It felt like the trees were trying to drag her backward, and she struggled with all her might to stay out of their clutches.

After a few minutes of running, she figured she must be getting close. Suddenly, she was flying through the air.

"Ouch!" she cried.

She opened her eyes to see that she was flat on her back, her arms and legs stretched out like a starfish. What had happened? Grace tilted her head back, her eyes following the path of her outstretched arm. Her pack was tangled up in the branches of a tree. Her arm was caught in the strap and she couldn't move it. *Great!*

Reaching over her head with her free arm, she grabbed one of the dangling straps and jerked it hard. There was a ripping sound, but it didn't come loose. That's when she heard it—a voice. And it was close.

"I don't see them, Hank. Double back and start over."

Grace could see a tall man through the trees. He was dressed in blue. Oh no, one of the security goons from the strip mine! Or was it Stuckless again? She lay on the ground, helpless. She was a sitting duck!

Every second seemed like an eternity. Grace held her breath, her heartbeat pounding in her ears. A branch moved nearby. She closed her eyes. *This is it! I'm done for!* she thought.

But then, the second she was sure she'd be discovered, the guard's footsteps crunched on the gravel, heading away from her. Grace let out her breath, but had no time to relax. She tried again to tug the strap free. *Her knife!* Lightning fast, she grabbed the knife from her pocket and slashed through the twisted strap. She jumped to her feet and took off through the trees. Within minutes, she found Mai in a clearing and rushed to her side.

"Mai, it's okay," she said. "I'm here." She reached out and grabbed Mai's shoulders. One of their caving ropes was twisted in Mai's hands. "What are you doing?"

"He f-f-fell into that sinkhole!" Mai sobbed, gesturing with the rope toward a gaping hole a few metres from them. "It's all my fault! I teased him—said he'd fall—that he'd g-gush blood."

"It's not your fault," Grace said gently, taking the rope from Mai's shaking hands and securing it around a tree with a sturdy knot. "You know Fred," she gulped, forcing a grin, "he's got a head like a rock. He'll be okay."

Wrapping the rope around her hand and holding it tight for balance, Grace leaned out over the hole and looked down. Her breath caught in her throat.

Fred wasn't moving!

Chapter

II

NO, NO, NO! THIS CAN'T BE HAPPENING!

Using the rope, Grace eased down into the pit, rappelling against the wall. Mai followed, holding the rope while Grace spotted her. As soon as Mai's feet touched the ground, she and Grace rushed over to Fred. His eyes were closed, but his chest was moving up and down—and there was no gushing blood.

Mai leaned over him and gently sprinkled water from her bottle onto his white face.

His eyes slowly fluttered open. "What happened?"

"You don't remember?" Grace said. "You fell. Lucky for you this wasn't one of those crazy deep sinkholes."

"Huh! Well it sure feels like it was," he moaned, staring upward. "Looks like the Grand Canyon from down here!"

"I think you just got the wind knocked out of you... and a scratch," Mai said.

Fred struggled to a sitting position. He wiggled around and pulled his pack from underneath him. "Hey Mai, it looks like my choco stash broke my fall! Nice and cushy soft."

"Geez, Fred, are you *ever* serious?" Grace shook her head.

Fred stared up at them with a lopsided grin, his unruly black curls falling over one eye. "Hungry?" he asked, holding up a squished chocolate cake.

Mai knelt down beside him. "Hungry? All you think about is food! You're lucky you didn't break your leg, you klutzy nincompoop," she chastised him as she pulled out her first-aid kit. "It's because of you I've had to refill my kit a dozen times." She proceeded to clean his cut like a pro.

Fred seemed to be enjoying himself. By the goofy look on his face, it was obvious he loved the attention from Nurse Mai.

"There," Mai finally sighed. "You're as good as new. Well, as good as you get, anyway."

Fred grabbed Grace and Mai's outstretched hands and they slowly pulled him to his feet. He shook out one arm then the other and repeated the action with both legs, looking like a demented scarecrow covered in twigs and leaves. "Everything's working a-okay," he said. "Let's get outta here."

"Sure, but we have to be careful. There's security everywhere!" warned Grace.

First Mai and then Fred slowly climbed back up the rope. Grace stood alone in the cavern, scanning the ground around her. Had her dad been here that day? she wondered. She took out her map and looked at the section she had folded to the front. This might be the PA3 sinkhole, the one her dad had been talking about.

PA stood for Point Aconi. The numbers were for each of the sinkholes her dad had found. PA3 was the third sinkhole at Point Aconi. Her dad had used the same type of coding for sites as they used to code the fossils at the fossil museum.

"Grace, come on," Mai called down from above.

"Just give me a sec!" Grace shouted back. She swept the beam of her flashlight around the cavern. Grace had been in the PA1 and PA2 sinkholes before with her dad. But back then they couldn't get farther than the PA2 because the tunnel leading away from it had been blocked by a cave-in.

Grace swung her beam to the left. A large pile of collapsed rubble obstructed the tunnel in one direction. *That must be the way back to the PA2*, she thought. It was probably the same pile of rock she and her dad had seen from the other side. All the sinkholes in this area seemed to run along this same tunnel. She continued in a circle until her light shone down the empty darkness of an unobstructed path in the opposite direction.

Suddenly Grace felt a gentle pull on the rope she'd tied around her waist. "C'mon, we gotta go!" Mai's voice sounded panicked.

"I'm just looking around," Grace responded.

"The guards could be coming!" Fred called.

"Okay!" Grace was about to turn and climb back out of the sinkhole when her light flashed on something against the wall a few metres down the tunnel. *Could it be?*

"Grace!" Fred yelled. "What are you doing? We're pulling you up!"

Grace dropped her flashlight and lunged toward the object. Her hands grabbed it just as she felt the sharp tug of the rope. "Got it!" she said. She clutched her newfound treasure to her chest and let herself get dragged back through the opening and pulled into the air.

Within minutes, she was back up on solid ground. Fred and Mai were both huffing and puffing from pulling her up, but apparently they still had enough air in their lungs to argue with each other.

"Fred, are you *crazy*? You could have a concussion. We're *not* staying!" Mai said, hands on her hips. "Right, Grace?"

Grace didn't answer. She plopped down on the ground and rested her treasure on her lap. She could hardly believe what she had found. She felt dizzy as she flipped up the front flap of her dad's field bag.

"*Grace,* we're going home, aren't we?" Mai said loudly. "Hey, what did you find?" She knelt beside her.

"It's my dad's bag—the one he always took with him fossil-hunting." Her voice cracked as she ran her hands gently over the worn leather.

"You mean he was here?" Mai gasped.

Grace nodded, opening his map and examining the notations. She searched the rest of the bag, pulling out his battered old rock hammer and some other tools. There was a fossil tucked in a side pouch.

"What does this mean?" Fred asked.

"That he was here that day, the day he disappeared," Grace said.

"But you knew that already," Mai said.

"Yeah..."

"It doesn't mean he didn't go back to the museum, does it?" Fred asked.

"No," Grace admitted. "But what happened to stop him from taking it? He'd never leave it behind!" She carefully repacked the bag and slung it over her shoulder. "If we found this, we might find something else."

"We can come back on Saturday," Mai said reassuringly.

Grace stood up. "I'm grounded on Saturday. We should go back down there now."

"I can't believe it!" Mai exclaimed, looking shocked. "Fred's hurt. Don't you care?"

Of course she cared. How could Mai say that?

"We've always done whatever you wanted," Mai continued. "Fred goes into tunnels even though he always

ends up getting hurt. We sneak out, lie to our parents...
and that's okay because we're your friends. But this—"

"I—" Grace started.

"Fred could've died." Mai was shaking as she pointed
down into the sinkhole. "We shouldn't even be here."

"Mai—"

Suddenly there was a rustling in the trees. "Oh no,
the security goons!" Fred cried. "Hide!"

Chapter
12

THERE WAS NOWHERE TO HIDE. GRACE FELT LIKE SCREAMING AS she stood frozen, hypnotized by the moving leaves. It was like a scene from a movie, like she was waiting for the monster to burst out and attack any second.

But it wasn't a monster that stepped into the clearing.

"Grace! Where were you? How come you ran off?" Jeeter said testily as he emerged from the foliage.

"What do you mean, where was *I*?" Grace shot back. "You're the one who disappeared."

"I thought you were behind me." Jeeter looked at Fred. His eyebrows shot up as he took in Fred's mud pie face and dead-leaf accessories. "Looks like I missed some action."

"*You!*" Fred exclaimed suddenly. "It was *you*."

Grace and Mai gaped at Fred. "What are you talking about?" Mai said.

Fred pointed an accusing finger at Jeeter. "*You* pushed me into that sinkhole!"

"Me?" Jeeter said. "He thinks *I* pushed him? I wasn't even here!"

"I thought you couldn't remember what happened?" Mai said, staring at Fred in horror.

"It just came back to me," Fred replied.

"You saw Jeeter push you?" Grace asked.

"I didn't exactly *see* him," muttered Fred. He was examining the ground as if there was something very interesting there.

"What do you mean, not exactly?" asked Mai.

"Well, *someone* had to push me. It's not like I just fell in for no reason." Fred scowled in accusation at Jeeter.

"Where were you anyway, Jeeter?" Grace asked.

"I followed Stuckless...but then I lost him," Jeeter responded. "Maybe *he* pushed you," he said sarcastically to Fred. "Or more likely you tripped!"

Grace sighed. It was crazy to think that Jeeter would try to hurt Fred, wasn't it? Besides, Fred *was* the biggest klutz in the universe. He probably tripped over his dumb baggy jeans, like always. What a mess.

"We don't have time for this," Jeeter continued. "That Stuckless guy and his buddies could find us any second. Are we even on public property?"

"Probably not," Grace admitted. "I really don't know how much land the strip mine company is leasing now." She looked out over the terrain. "Maybe all of it..."

"Well, if we're trespassing, we'd better get outta here," Jeeter said.

Grace clutched her dad's field bag to her chest. "Maybe you're right."

Suddenly a new voice crackled in the air. "Hello? Grace? Is anybody there?"

Now what? Grace wondered. "Jessica? It's Grace. What's up?"

"I gotta bail. The coach called my mom about me missing swim practice. She just called me on my cell phone and I'm totally busted. Favour's over. But don't worry—I was checking out the window. That Stuckless guy hasn't been around all day, so you're in the clear. Later!" With a final crackle, she was gone.

"C'mon." Jeeter motioned to them. "I know the way back."

Everyone followed Jeeter as he raced through the woods. They went as fast as they could until they arrived back at their bikes. Jeeter carefully circled around first to make sure the coast was clear.

"Okay," Grace panted, "let's get out of here. If my mom finds out I've been up here, I'm dead." She glanced nervously over her shoulder, expecting Stuckless to burst through the trees at any minute. "If we take the highway to North Sydney, we can hook onto Shore Road. It's a longer route, but no one will think we went that way."

"But it's already seven o'clock," Mai cautioned. "It'll be dark in a couple of hours. That's barely enough time if we go our normal route. If we go to North Sydney, it'll take twice as long to get home. Plus, that means we have to drive by, you know..."

"Of course I know!" Grace snapped. "I wouldn't go that way unless I had to!"

"Why are you yelling at *me?* It's not my fault we're out here." Mai's feet fumbled on the pedals of her bike. Then she took off, her pack flapping loosely on the back.

"Mai, wait!" Grace called.

"Nice going, Grace!" Fred shook his head, then sped after Mai.

Why did I yell like that? Grace scolded herself. *I didn't mean to.* She rubbed her temples. Things just kept getting worse. "Can you follow them and make sure they get home okay?" she asked Jeeter.

"Who's going to make sure *you* get home okay?" he responded.

"I can take care of myself. Besides, if Stuckless knows I was out here, I'm already in bags of trouble. He'll tell my mom for sure this time. It's no good if you get grounded too."

"You're not going anywhere by yourself. Stuckless likely doesn't know for sure that we were here. If he found our bikes, he would have taken them."

"You're probably right," Grace conceded.

"We'll take the shorter route back, but we'll both watch out for Stuckless," Jeeter said. "And don't worry about me. I don't get grounded."

*   *   *

As it turned out, it *was* dark when Grace and Jeeter finally reached Sydney Mines. They hadn't seen Stuckless at all on their way back. Jeeter rode with Grace to her street and then continued home. As she stood in the driveway, Grace looked up at the dark windows. The thought of being alone in an empty house was not appealing.

She closed her eyes and hugged her dad's field bag. The lilac hedges her grandmother had planted around the house were in bloom and the delicious perfume filled her nostrils. Lilacs meant June, which meant school would be over soon. She used to get so excited for the fossil-hunting trips she'd take with her dad over summer break. Not this year.

Overwhelmed by a sudden urge to see the spot where the accident happened, she found herself pedalling down Huron Avenue and onto Richard Street. She turned onto Shore Road and coasted by homes that were now abandoned, decorated with condemned signs and broken windows. Their once-manicured lawns were now minimeadows, where the weeds grew waist-high. Everything looked neglected under the pale light of the flickering street lamps.

Shore Road used to be the main thoroughfare between Sydney Mines and North Sydney. But erosion and bootleg mines had eaten away the cliffs and now the road drooped dangerously low in spots. Hardly anyone used it anymore. All the people who lived along the road had been relocated, like in Point Aconi.

As Grace approached the Fraser Avenue intersection, she stopped pedalling. There it was—the spot.

Grace couldn't resist. She slid off her bike and walked it over to the shoulder. She gazed down at the water. Moonlight danced on the ocean waves. She and her dad had gone fossil-hunting below on the beach at Sutherland's Corner. The steep path down to the shore was only a few hundred metres from where she stood. They had probably even walked along the beach under this very spot.

Grace laid her bike in the grass and ran her hands over the smooth guardrail at the side of the road. They had replaced it shortly after the accident, but not before Grace had snuck out to see it the morning after. She shuddered at the memory of the ripped and twisted metal.

She climbed over the rail and sat down gingerly on the curved metal edge. Her legs dangled and her feet brushed the tips of the grass. A warm breeze ruffled her hair as a whirring June bug droned past. What if the note was true? If it hadn't been an accident, what did that mean?

The police report had said that her dad's car had lost control at the bottom of Fraser Avenue, where it intersected with Shore Road. It was where the old Hartigan coal mine had been. They'd attributed it to poor road conditions due to torrential rains. *A tragic accident*, the papers had called it.

Grace gripped the guardrail with one hand and leaned over the edge. She tried to see the rocks below, but couldn't. How far was it? If he *had* been in the car, could he have gotten out somehow? She'd seen lots of movies where people got amnesia from accidents and didn't remember who they were. What if that had happened to her dad and he was somewhere out there, alone and afraid?

Suddenly the road lit up brightly behind her. Someone was coming! Grace ducked behind the guardrail and peeked out between the metal slats.

The vehicle slowed down. Her body tensed. It was Stuckless's truck and there was someone with him in the passenger seat. Her heart was playing the drums on her ribs.

The passenger turned and Grace saw the outline of a cap on his head. There was something familiar about him, but she couldn't place what it was. He reached up and turned on the overhead light, but his face was hidden in shadow.

Grace gasped. Her eyes had to be playing tricks on her. The hat the passenger was wearing—she could read it as plain as day. *DAL!*

Chapter
13

"DAD?" SHE WHISPERED, REACHING HER HAND OUT TOWARD the truck.

The passenger turned the interior light off and the truck continued on, turning up Fraser Avenue. At that same moment the moon turned off too, hidden behind a cloud. It was like Grace had been suddenly blindfolded.

Grace leapt after the car, forgetting the guardrail was in her way. She banged into the metal slats and stumbled backward. There was only a metre or so between the guardrail and the cliff face. She gasped as her foot slipped. The earth was falling away beneath her.

She was at the edge!

Grace lost her balance and fell forward. Her face smacked into the dirt. She could feel her legs dangling in the air behind her.

She tried to wriggle forward. But as soon as she started moving, she could feel more earth eroding away beneath her legs. *She was going to fall!*

She desperately felt around for something to grab onto. The guardrail was too far away. Her rock hammer! She could use it to dig into the ground and climb to safety. Where was her pack? She'd dropped it beside her when she'd sat down. Her eyes were starting to adjust to the sudden darkness and she could see faint outlines.

There it was!

She clenched one hand tightly around a clump of grass and stretched the other toward her pack. Her fingertips brushed the strap, but she couldn't quite grab it. Her other hand slipped on the grass.

She wasn't going to make it!

Dad, help me! she screamed in her head.

A pair of hands grabbed her. "Come on, Grace! Climb!" her rescuer yelled, pulling her upward.

She reached up to grab his arms, and used all her strength to climb up. Suddenly she was on solid ground again. Gasping, she lay against the rail. Her rescuer was stretched out beside her, his ragged breathing matching her own.

At that moment the moon reappeared and Grace turned to her knight in shining armour. "Dad?" She stopped. "*Jeeter*? What are you doing here?"

"Who were you expecting?" Jeeter grumbled. "You're welcome, by the way. You know, for saving your life."

"I was fine," she muttered, feeling her face flush.

"Uh-huh." Jeeter stood up and tugged Grace to her feet.

She brushed the dirt off her clothes, fingering a tear in her jeans. "How did you know I was here?"

"I wanted to tell you something. By the time I came back around the corner, I saw you biking away. So I followed you."

"Why?"

"Wherever you were going in the dark, I wasn't going to let you go by yourself." He peered down at her. "What are you doing here?"

"I just felt like I had to come here. Finding my dad's bag today...I don't know, I needed to see the spot...where it happened." Grace brushed a tear from her eye. "Anyways, thanks...for pulling me up."

"No sweat. You can save me some day," Jeeter replied. "Ready to go?"

She nodded.

The grabbed their bikes and turned back toward town.

"Are you sure you're okay?" Jeeter asked as they slowly pedalled home. "It sounded like you called me 'Dad' back there. I thought you must be sleepwalking or something!"

Grace told him about seeing the man with the Dalhousie hat in Stuckless's truck.

"You think it was your dad's hat?" Jeeter asked.

"I don't know." Grace stopped her bike and sat back on the seat. "Dad was wearing it that day." She rubbed her temples. "I've never seen anyone else wearing one."

"But how would the guy with Stuckless get it? Could the other guy have been Stanley? Do they know each other?"

"Know each other? Well, the other guy did look familiar.... Oh, I don't know!" Frustrated, she gazed down the hill behind her at Shore Road. "Nothing makes sense anymore!"

"What do you mean?"

"When I was sitting on the guardrail I remembered something. I don't know why I didn't think of it before. Everything was crazy, I guess."

"What was it?"

"Dad would never have willingly driven on Shore Road. He always said it wasn't safe, because of the erosion." She pointed to the droops in the pavement. "He was convinced it would all fall into the Atlantic one day. He called it a death trap. Whenever we drove to North Sydney, we always went a different way. I never really thought about it, until now."

Jeeter frowned. "So why would he go on Shore Road that day? And then he just happened to have a car accident? That *is* weird!"

"Maybe he knew it would happen someday, a feeling. That could be why he never trusted the road.... Geez, now I really sound crazy!" she sighed, closing her eyes.

"It's been hard on you."

"It's just that my head hasn't stopped spinning since that mystery guy put the note in my locker. It won't turn off. Who was he? Why didn't he tell me to my face? If he knows it wasn't an accident, why didn't he go to the police?"

"Maybe he couldn't."

"Why not?"

"I don't know, but I'm sure you'll figure it out, Grace," Jeeter said. "You're really smart."

"I don't feel very smart."

"Well, think about it. What if his accident *did* have something to do with his work at the fossil museum?" Jeeter said.

"Or...maybe it had something to do with the strip mines? Lots of people were mad about the protests he organized. But then...that wasn't new. He was always against strip mining." Grace swallowed and kneaded the handlebars of her bike. "Everything was fine that morning—I mean, we had pancakes..."

They rode the rest of the way home in silence and coasted to a stop in front of Grace's house on Queen Street.

"So what did you want to tell me, anyways?" Grace asked.

Jeeter looked startled. "What?"

"You know, when you said before that you came back to find me because you needed to tell me something?"

"Oh, that!" Jeeter glanced down at the fossil bag Grace was clutching in her arms. "Never mind...it can wait."

"Are you sure?"

Jeeter hesitated for a second. "Forget it. I'd better get going. If you can't sleep and want to talk later, call me." He sped away and disappeared around the turn.

Grace went inside and hobbled up the stairs. She slid her jeans off and examined the rip in the thigh. They were a total write-off. There was a long, deep scrape on her leg to match the hole in her pants. *That needs peroxide*, she thought, and she headed to the bathroom to clean off her wound.

As she entered the washroom, she caught a glimpse of herself in the mirror and gasped. Her face was covered in tiny scratches from the tree branches. *Great!* she thought sarcastically.

She washed her face gently, hoping the scratches would disappear overnight. After cleaning the scrape on her leg, she crawled into bed, yawning deeply as she got under the covers.

Just then, Grace heard an engine. She tiptoed to the window and carefully pulled back the curtain, watching as Stuckless got out of his truck. He was alone now. He unlocked his door and paused in the open doorway. He turned and seemed to look directly at Grace's window. Grace jumped back. Did he see her? She waited a minute and peeked out again, but he was gone.

Grace returned to bed, her head filled with unanswered questions. Why had Stuckless been following her? Was this about the strip mines, after all? She thought about seeing Stuckless at the Halfway Road pit. How had he managed to get the mining lease for that area? What had he done?

She tried to sleep, but after hours of tossing and turning, she realized it was hopeless. Her mom had already come home and gone to bed.

Grace pulled out her walkie-talkie. Jeeter would help.

*   *   *

"What else was your dad working on? Maybe there's another site we could check," Jeeter suggested.

They'd been brainstorming, trying to make sense of everything.

"As far as I know, he was only working at Point Aconi. But if there was another site, it would be on his map." She pulled his field bag onto her lap and dug out his map. "Hold on a sec." There was a moment of silence as she examined his notes. "I'm looking at it right now," she finally said, "and there's nothing new here."

Jeeter's frustrated sigh echoed her own feelings. "How about his office in the basement? Maybe there are clues in there."

"Mom locked it and she can't find the key, but I'm going to find a way to get in there. I think Stanley might have been trying to get in there when he was over for dinner—"

"WHAT?" Jeeter's voice vibrated through the air. "He was *in your house*?"

"Yeah...Mom invited him after he found her when her car broke down on the side of the road, but that's another story. Sorry I didn't mention it. I told Mai—I guess you weren't there. She didn't seem to think it was a big deal."

"He actually tried to break into your dad's office? I can't *believe* it!"

"Well, I don't know that for sure. It seemed like he was trying to get into the basement. And the only thing down there is my dad's office.... Hang on, how did you know he had an office in the basement?"

"Uh, I don't know. I guess I just assumed he'd have one…Roger does."

"Oh."

"Grace, you have to get into that office!"

Chapter

14

GRACE COULD HEAR HER MOTHER'S SHOWER GOING AS SHE tromped down into the kitchen the next morning. She was chugging some orange juice out of the container when her eyes spied the calendar on the fridge.

Her mom was on an extra shift at the ferry terminal this morning. *Yes!* Grace thought. This was the perfect time to look for the office key and then sneak in. But how would she get out of school? Pacing back and forth, it came to her—*sick day.* She'd definitely need some convincing symptoms, though. Her mom was tough to fool.

Fever? No, too hard. Hmmm...stomach cramps? Iffy.

Where was Fred when she needed him? He'd have loads of suggestions—he could probably make her look almost dead. Suddenly it was like Fred's genius in the ways of all things crazy spoke to her.

Vomit!

And the quickest way to make herself vomit was to eat peanut butter. Brilliant! The only problem was that she'd actually have to eat it. She shuddered, totally grossed out at the thought. Well, this was an emergency and it called for drastic measures. She was only a little allergic, anyway—not the drop-dead kind, just the barf-'til-your-insides-are-outside kind.

There wasn't much time. She dropped a bagel in the toaster and waited for it to pop. Then she grabbed the peanut butter and spread it on the bagel, watching as the gooey brown substance oozed over the sides. Baby poop. That's what it looked like. Her stomach flipped and rolled. She felt like she was going to barf and she hadn't even eaten it yet.

The shower stopped. *Crap!* Her Mom would be down any minute to make coffee. She stared at the brown goo. It was now or never. Closing her eyes, she bit a chunk off the bagel—and gagged. *Keep it together,* she told herself. *Think happy thoughts. You're on the beach. It's summer. The water is blue—no, it's brown goo! Yeeeuckk! Who am I kidding? Swallow! Swallow now!*

The poo-covered bagel fell into her belly like a rock. Her stomach was *not* happy about it. She tossed the rest in the garbage and threw a paper towel overtop to hide the evidence.

Her mother's footsteps echoed on the stairs. Grace's face felt clammy and she lifted her hand to—*oh, double crap! Her face!* She'd forgotten it was covered in scratches from her run through the woods the day before. If her mom saw those, she'd be totally busted. Bending forward so her hair draped like a curtain over her eyes, Grace clutched her gurgling stomach and raced past her mother on the stairs.

"Grace, what in heaven's name—?"

She barely made it. Slamming the bathroom door shut, the geyser started when she was still a metre from the toilet. Good thing she aimed right. It didn't stop—it kept coming and coming and coming....

"Uhhh," she moaned. She rested her head on her arms, which were draped across the toilet seat. The taste of vomit filled her mouth. Maybe this hadn't been such a great idea, after all.

Her mother knocked on the door. "Grace, you've been in there a long time. Are you okay?"

Grace mumbled something indecipherable between retches.

"I can't hear you. I'm coming in," her mother said as she opened the door.

Grace buried her head deeper in the bowl to hide her face. "Mom, I think I have the flu," she groaned.

"You poor baby. Maybe I could get someone to take my shift this morning."

"No!" Grace yelled a bit too eagerly. "I mean, no, that's okay. I'll be fine."

"Well..." Her mother paused.

Grace thought she could feel her mother's eyes trying to see through the toilet bowl.

"I don't like the thought of you being here alone when you're sick. Get into bed and I'll be back up in a few minutes to check on you." Her mother closed the door.

Grace listened to her mom's footsteps on the stairs. Sighing, she realized the barfing had finally stopped. Phase One was complete. She looked at herself in the mirror. *Not* good. The scratches on her face looked like trails of angry fire ants on her still-pasty, post-puking-white skin. *Camouflage,* she thought. *I need camouflage.* Teasing her hair into a tangled rat's nest, she pulled it down to cover her face and checked out the effect. *Perfect.* Her mom wouldn't be able to see a thing through that mop.

"Sweetie, I'm bringing you up some juice," her mother called from downstairs.

Grace jumped into bed, pulling the covers up to hide most of her head. When her mother came in, she peered over the edge of the comforter.

"Here you are, honey," Grace's mother cooed, putting

the juice on the nightstand and sitting down beside her. "What about if I stay home? We could curl up on the couch and both have a sick day. I've got a Royal Winnipeg Ballet performance taped."

Ballet? No way! Her mom was in gushy-gooey mode. Grace felt like she was going to barf all over again.

Grace peeked out from under her hair jungle. "I'm feeling a little better, Mom. You should go to work."

"Well, I'll wait for a while and see how you do," her mom said, looking disappointed. "Try to get some rest and I'll check in on you in a little bit."

Great! Now she was trapped in her room. Every minute was agony.

It was another two hours before her mom reappeared, all dressed for work. She sat down on the edge of Grace's bed and patted the covers. Her nails were now a shocking coral colour.

"How are you feeling?" she asked, her voice filled with concern. "Do you want me to stay with you? Eleanor said she'd cover the rest of my shift."

"No, it's okay, Mom," Grace said. "I'll be all right. What if I call every hour or so and leave a message on your cell? That way you'll know I'm fine."

Her mother stood up and ran her hands down the front of her pants, smoothing out the creases. "All right, Grace. I'm only ten minutes away if you need me. Are you sure you're okay?" She reached down as if to brush Grace's hair from her face.

Grace burrowed deeper and let out a huge burp. "Oops, sorry! Yup, I'm sure. I'll be fine."

Her mother frowned and pulled her hand away. Gushy-gooey mom had disappeared as quickly as she'd come. "Fine. Remember, every hour."

Grace waited to hear the car door, then raced to the window to make sure her mother had driven away. She quickly got dressed and attempted to brush her hair. "Ow, ow, *ow!*" she howled as she tried to yank her way through the knots. The brush got stuck in the tangled mass and it took five minutes of tugging and screaming to get it out again. Grace looked into the mirror and grimaced at her reflection. *Beautiful!* she thought. *Fire-ant face and tumbleweed hair!*

*　　*　　*

Equipped with her flashlight, Grace opened the basement door and peered down into the pitch black. She reached over to flick on the light switch, but nothing happened. The light really was out. Stanley had been telling the truth about that.

The damp smell of dirt and coal filled her nostrils as she descended into the darkness. *This feels like fossil-hunting in the tunnels*, she thought.

Grace felt something brush against her arm.

"Aaahhhh!" she screamed, jumping back and swatting at it. She swung the beam of light toward her arm, but she couldn't see anything. *It must've been a cobweb.* Grace shuddered. Cobwebs meant *spiders.*

She waved the beam back and forth as she tiptoed through the darkness, now looking for *two* things—the door and *spiders.*

Thump!

Grace froze on the stairs. *That was no spider.*

Thump!

What was it? She swung the beam in a wild arc around the room.

Thump!

The sound was coming from *above* her. Heart sputtering, she slowly tiptoed back up toward the kitchen. What if it was Stuckless here to kidnap her? Or worse?

"Hello?" she croaked, terror squeezing her vocal cords.

Hello? You're saying hello to your murderer? Say something tough. Be fierce.

"I, um, I've got my dad's *gun*. It's loaded!" She poked her head around the corner, eyes cemented shut. "And he, uh, took me to the firing range so I know how to use it!" she yelled. *Open your eyes, you dork!*

Grace peered around the doorway into the kitchen. Nothing. She held her flashlight up over her shoulder like a baseball bat and slid on her sock feet across the hardwood floor, stealthily making her way to the living room.

THUMP!

Grace dove behind the couch. The sounds were coming from the direction of the window. She inched forward on her hands and knees and peered around the corner.

Someone was there!

Chapter
15

"CLIMBING IN THE WINDOW—BRILLIANT IDEA," THE INTRUDER MUT-
tered. "I probably broke my foot!"

That doesn't sound like a murderer, Grace thought to
herself. "Who's there?" she demanded, leaping from behind the coach, flashlight ready.

The intruder spun around. He still had one foot on
the windowsill and as he turned he fell to the floor with
a thud. "What the—?!" he hollered, staring up at her.
"What happened to your face?"

"*Jeeter?*" Grace lowered her flashlight. "You scared me
to death! What are you doing here?"

"I thought you could use some help." He examined
her face and hair. "I guess I was right—you don't look
so good."

"Thanks a lot. I thought you were my psycho neighbour, here to kill me. Why didn't you knock?"

"I tried that. And you didn't answer the doorbell either." He stood up, rubbing his ankle.

"So you break into houses when people don't answer
the door?"

"You screamed. I thought you were in trouble! But it was just you being your klutzy self, huh?"

Grace scowled. "No, there was a—" she broke off. *Hmm...he probably won't think much of me screaming at imaginary spiders,* she thought.

"What?"

"Never mind!"

"Great," Jeeter said. "Got anything to eat? I'm starving!"

Grace led him into the kitchen. Jeeter searched the cupboards and pulled out a bag of chips. He ripped it open and popped a chip into his mouth. Grace laughed as his face scrunched up like he'd swallowed a tablespoon of salt. Holding the bag up, he exclaimed, *"All natural guacamole soy chips?* Yuck! You eat this stuff?"

"Not really," Grace answered. "My mom went a little psycho when Dad.... Anyway, she was on this total organic kick. It was *torture.* Lucky it didn't last long. I think she hated that stuff more than I did."

Jeeter rifled through the rest of the food in her cupboards. "Unsalted cashews, pomegranate juice, banana chips, dried apricots...kill me now," he groaned. "Okay, forget the food! Have you checked out your dad's office yet?"

"I was *trying* to do that when you broke in," Grace responded. "C'mon." She gestured for him to follow her.

They stopped at the top of the stairs and stared down into the gloom. "You go first," Grace said, nudging Jeeter's arm.

"Doesn't the light work?" he asked, flipping the switch up and down.

"Nope." Grace clicked on her flashlight and passed it to him. "Here, take this."

Jeeter swung the beam in front of them and took a step.

Creeeaaaak! The top step groaned in complaint.

Grace followed cautiously. Suddenly, the flashlight beam caught a dark object hovering in front of their faces.

"Aaaahh!" Grace screamed, burying her face in Jeeter's back.

"Grace!" he cried. "You're pushing me!"

"Spider!" she wailed, peeking over his shoulder. She wrapped her hands around his waist.

Jeeter brushed the spider away with the tip of the flashlight. It scurried up the side of the wall and disappeared into the dark.

"There, it's gone," he said over his shoulder. "How about loosening your death grip?"

"Sorry," Grace muttered.

"Nothing to be scared of," he said, continuing his descent. "They're not poisonous, you know."

"I don't like spiders!"

"I figured," he laughed.

They slowly inched their way forward in the dark, the beam lighting a thin path through towering piles of boxes.

When they reached Grace's dad's office at the far end of the basement, Grace eagerly reached out and grabbed the doorknob.

"Darn, it *is* locked!"

"So where do you think your mom hid the key?"

"I don't know. I've been racking my brain—and Mom's, too. She has no clue where she left it!"

"She'd likely put it someplace she thought would be easy to remember. Do you keep a key outside?"

"Yeah, for the back door. In case we forget ours. I mean, in case I forget mine...I've done that a few times." Grace scrunched up her face. "It's under the flowerpot."

"Maybe she did the same thing down here."

They looked, but there weren't any flowerpots in the basement. So they checked under buckets of paint, an old sled, totes filled with Christmas decorations, broken skis—even her ancient deflated kiddie pool. All they found were lots and lots of spiders.

Then Grace noticed a bag of soil mix leaning against the wall. *Hmm...soil goes* in *the flowerpots*, she thought to herself. *It's worth a try.* She lifted up the bag.

"I found it!" she cried, holding up a metal key. She carried it over to her dad's office door and slowly inserted it into the lock—it fit perfectly. She turned the key and the door clicked open.

Grace flicked the switch and light spilled out from the open door. As she stepped inside her dad's office, she felt an emptiness in the bottom of her stomach. She wasn't prepared for the sadness that overwhelmed her. Teetering stacks of papers and books covered every surface. *Dad never was one for filing stuff,* she thought to herself fondly.

"Whew, what a mess!" Jeeter's voice snapped Grace out of her reverie.

He plopped down in her dad's chair, shoving aside a stack of books.

"Don't touch that!" Grace motioned for him to move. "I'll do it."

"Sorry, Grace," Jeeter said. "I'm trying to help, remember?"

"I'm sorry I snapped," she sighed. "A little jumpy, I guess."

Grace and Jeeter examined reams of files and papers; topographical maps of Sydney Mines, Florence, and Point Aconi; and endless photos of fossils over the next hour. One whole stack of files related to the strip mines and the protests. Another pile contained information on the tar ponds project, mostly newspaper articles about the failed cleanup attempts and costs.

Grace's dad had done some consulting for one of the bidders on the project and had followed it closely, even after the company he'd worked for had lost the bid. But most of the data he'd been collecting just looked like stuff from the newspaper or downloaded from the internet. There was nothing top secret, that was for sure. Most of it had to do with a company called Sandstar Environmental Corporation, which had won the contract.

"We're not getting any closer to finding the answers!" Grace said in disgust.

"Be patient," Jeeter replied. "You'll figure it out." He leaned over and touched her arm.

"You should understand," Grace sniffed. "All this is just making me sadder. It feels like I can hardly breathe most of the time—like there's a boulder on my chest. It's no use!"

"I know it's hard," Jeeter said. "You miss him."

Grace nodded. "If only something would work out..." She shuffled through another stack of papers. "Forget it—there's nothing here!" Disappointment washed over her.

"Wait!" Jeeter stood up, waving a piece of paper at her. "There's something here with Stanley's name on it."

It was a page ripped from a memo pad with a hand-written note:

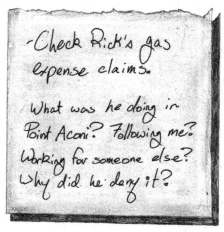

-Check Rick's gas expense claims.

What was he doing in Point Aconi? Following me? Working for someone else? Why did he deny it?

"What does it mean?" Jeeter asked as he leaned over her shoulder.

"I don't know. Stanley always complained he was broke. What if he was doing something he wasn't supposed to and my dad found out? Like cheating on his expenses? I mean, Point Aconi, that's where my dad was… but this doesn't look like Dad's handwriting."

Brrrinnngg!!!

The phone rang upstairs. Grace had forgotten to call her mom like she'd promised. *Great, more trouble,* she thought. She stuffed the note in her pocket and raced up the stairs, grabbing the receiver just as the phone was about to go to voicemail. "Hi, Mom—"

"Grace, it's me, Fred. Listen, I have something really important to tell you, but we have to meet in person. You're gonna go nuts. I couldn't believe it myself. I mean, I knew there was something weird going on, but I never thought he'd—"

"Fred—*slow down*! What are you talking about?"

"I had to use the pay phone 'cause I can't find my walkie-talkie. It's Jeeter. He left school. I was worried he would go to your place. Whatever you do, *don't* let him in. You can't trust him!"

Grace heard the basement door close behind her and turned slowly to see Jeeter walking toward her. She was glued to the spot, afraid to move.

"What's wrong?" Jeeter asked, a puzzled expression on his face.

Grace's eyes locked with Jeeter's as Fred's voice whispered urgently in her ear, "Grace, did you hear me? Jeeter's dangerous!"

Chapter
16

"GRACE?" FRED WHISPERED AGAIN.

"Sure, Mom. See you then." Grace felt numb as she clicked the phone back in its holder. "That was Mom," she lied. "She'll be home any minute. You'd better go."

"Well, I guess I'll see you tomorrow," Jeeter said, walking towards the door. "Call me tonight if you want..."

As soon as he closed the door behind him, Grace's casual stance disappeared and she ran to turn the deadlock into place. She let out the breath she was holding and leaned her head against the frame. What was going on?

Grace spent the afternoon in her room, trying to make sense of the flurry of thoughts flying through her head. What was Fred talking about on the phone? Was Jeeter really dangerous? Or had Fred's jealousy just got the best of him? And why hadn't Fred just said what he wanted to on the phone?

It wasn't until Grace heard her mother's car door slam that she remembered her other problem—her face. She flew to the bathroom mirror, hoping for a miracle. No such luck. The fire-ant-like trails of scratches were as red as ever. She had to hide them!

She rummaged through her mom's gazillion bottles of beauty products and makeup stuff, looking for a disguise. What could she use? She plucked a jar from the back of the drawer and read the label: *Blue Algae Soothing Sea Mask. Hmm...*she thought, *soothing...and blue. That should do the trick.* She scooped it out in handfuls and slathered the entire jar over her face. *Perfect!* She was a lovely shade of blue—and there wasn't a scratch in sight.

She bounded down the stairs to confront Mother the Inquisitor.

"Good heavens, Grace! What on earth is the matter with your face?" her mom asked the second she saw her.

"It's for breakouts."

"You mean pimples?" her mother asked, her eyebrows raised. "I've never noticed any on you."

"I get them all the time."

"Well, I brought us a treat since you were stuck inside all day. Fish and chips—I know how much you love this stuff!" Her mother smiled, holding up two bags of takeout. "I was guessing your *flu* would be over by now?"

Grace didn't have the heart to tell her mother that fish and chips had been her dad's favourite takeout, not hers. Grace had always ordered chicken fingers.

They ate in silence. Grace did her best to choke down the slimy fish and chips. The odd drop of blue algae sea mask didn't add much to the taste, either.

The rest of the evening passed pretty much without incident, if you didn't count Grace's mother's constant glances at her blue face or her annoying "Are you planning on wearing that stuff all night?" comments every half-hour. Unfortunately, Grace had no choice but to keep the mask on. Her mother was in the gooiest of her gushy-gooey moods and was stuck to her like tree sap.

By the second hour of the Royal Winnipeg Ballet her mother had taped, Grace was getting a bit worried. Her face had started tingling—and not in a good way.

"You know," said Grace's mom during a particularly boring part of the ballet, "since you're worried about your complexion these days, maybe I can help a bit with something else." She held up one of Grace's hands. They both looked down at her stubby chewed-off nails. "How about a little manicure?"

"There's nothing wrong with my nails, Mom." Grace snatched her hand back. "I'm no ballerina and I never will be."

Her mother frowned and withdrew back to her side of the couch. Neither one spoke for a while.

Meanwhile, Grace's face was getting hotter by the minute. She was squirming so much her mother was bound to notice something was up. This blue stuff had to come off, like, *now*. She opened her mouth to spurt out some lame excuse to escape when her mother beat her to it.

"Now I know what's different about you tonight, Grace. Aside from your under-the-sea hue and that awful hairdo. Your hat's missing—that thing is usually glued to your head. I miss seeing it. Where is it?"

Shoot! She hadn't thought of her mom noticing that. "Um, well, I'm not sure," Grace mumbled, trying to think of a good answer. "I think I might've lost it," she blurted out. *Not a good choice.*

Her mother froze, a stunned look on her face. "*Lost* it?" she finally said. "You *lost* it?"

"Well, not really. It's got to be around somewhere," Grace said, backpedalling. She couldn't say that Jessica had it—that would open a whole new can of worms.

Her mother's voice rose. "But it can't be gone. That was the last thing your father ever gave us—I mean you."

"Don't worry. I'll find it." Grace reached out and awkwardly patted her mom's shoulder. Why was her mom so upset? It was *her* hat, after all.

Her mom buried her head in her hands. "How could you be so irresponsible?"

"Sorry." Grace's heart plummeted to the pit of her stomach. It seemed like she couldn't do anything right these days.

Her mother leaned her head on Grace's shoulder. "Heavens, I don't know what came over me." She reached for a tissue and blew her nose, mumbling into her hand.

"Pardon?" Grace's attention was now split between her mother and her own searing-hot-inferno face.

"I said I know it's been hard for you too," she sniffed, dabbing her eyes. "We never really talk about it. I guess I just can't face it most of the time..." she trailed off, her voice filled with mother-guilt.

Grace couldn't take it anymore. She had to get the blue stuff off her face—*now!* "Well, I know what happened to Dad wasn't an accident," she blurted out. "Something happened to him and I'm going to find out what!" She turned and raced up the stairs, frantically rubbing at the blue goop as she ran, the vision of her mother's thunderstruck face burned into her brain.

Grace ran into the bathroom and stuck her head under the faucet, letting the cool water run over her molten skin. A whole layer of skin had probably melted off.

She opened one eye for a peek—not too bad, actually. Of course, she was now the shade of a ripe tomato, but the scratches from her forbidden excursion had blended in nicely.

Grace tiptoed back into her room and lay down on her bed. She couldn't believe she had let the cat out of the bag about her dad's accident like that. Her mother probably thought she was totally off her rocker. Now she'd be worried that Grace wasn't *moving forward* with her healing, or some other therapy junk.

She crawled under the covers. Fred still hadn't called her back. Maybe he was waiting to hear from her. She tried to reach him on the walkie-talkie, but didn't have any luck. Then she remembered he'd said he couldn't find his. She tried to call Mai as well, but didn't get an answer from her either. *Mai must still be mad*, she thought to herself.

Sighing, she rolled onto her back, gazing at the swirling galaxies above her. She thought about the note from her dad's office. It had mentioned Point Aconi. And she'd found his field bag out there too. It seemed everything was leading back there.

She tossed and turned for a long while, unable to get her mind off her father. Finally, she drifted off to an unsettled sleep, only to wake a few short hours later. Her alarm clock glowed 1:30 AM. The moon was low and it shimmered through the leaves of the big oak tree across the street and into her front bedroom window.

She flipped her walkie-talkie on to talk to Jeeter, then changed her mind, tossing it back into her pack. Frustrated, she flopped back onto her pillow and clicked on the wave machine that sat on her night table. Instantly, she felt herself relaxing, her breathing mimicking the pattern of the waves. She was just about to drift off again, when—

Kchhhh...

Muffled voices were coming from her backpack. Someone was on her walkie-talkie! Maybe Mai had forgiven her after all. She grabbed it and was about to hit the transmit button when she heard a voice.

"Things...out of hand," the voice said, "... can't find..." Only bits and pieces of what the person was saying were coming in between the bursts of static. The voice spoke again, "... kid is persistent...you know...than anyone...."

Was that Stuckless's voice? If so, who was he talking to? Grace looked at her walkie-talkie. It was on channel two, not one they normally used. She must have hit the wrong button when she thought she'd turned it off.

Grace crept to the side window and cautiously peeked over the sill. There was a faint green glow coming from Stuckless's basement window. She grabbed her binoculars from her pack and focused them for a closer look. Stuckless was sitting in front of a computer, talking into something...another walkie-talkie, maybe? A CB radio?

"Okay...you're sure...could be trouble..." he said. "...yes...tomorrow...." With a final crackle, the conversation ended.

Grace sat on the side of her bed, clutching her walkie-talkie tightly in her hands. The night had returned to its sleepy silence, but there was no sleeping for Grace. She stared with wide eyes out her window into the empty darkness. What was going on?

Even her wave machine wouldn't help her tonight.

Chapter
17

BY THE TIME GRACE WANDERED DOWNSTAIRS THE NEXT MORNING, it felt like she'd already been through a whole day. Her eyes watered as she yawned for the hundredth time. She didn't think she'd gotten any full hours of sleep time.

It had taken almost an entire bottle of her mom's fancy conditioner and endless tugs, yanks, and screams to get all the tangles out of her hair. She was convinced she'd left at least half her long blonde locks in the shower drain.

There was something to be said for algae, though. It seemed to have eaten up all the scratches on her face. Her skin had faded from ripe tomato to a pale orange colour. It looked like she'd washed her face in self-tanning lotion.

Grace walked into the kitchen as her mother was pouring her coffee.

Her mother looked at her strangely. "I've been doing some thinking..." she started.

Warning bells blared in Grace's head. Whatever her mom had to say, it wasn't going to be good. She grabbed her pack, scooped up a muffin, and headed for the door.

"Late for school!" she called over her shoulder, slamming the door behind her before her mother had a chance to look at the clock.

Grace hopped on her bike and decided to go to Jessica's. She swerved onto Clyde Avenue, then took a left on Beech Street. Minutes later she was reunited with her hat. She plopped her old friend back on top of her head and pulled her ponytail through the back.

She held her arms out at her sides and tipped her head back. She loved the feeling of the crisp wind zipping over her body, tugging at her clothes and filling her lungs.

As Grace whizzed across Main and zipped around another turn, she suddenly realized that she was almost at Mai's house on Crescent Street. *Traitor bike!* She sighed and veered into Mai's driveway. It was as good a time as any to eat crow and apologize. She wondered if Mai would even talk to her. Before she had a chance to knock on the door, it swung open and she was looking straight into Mai's startled brown eyes.

They stood there, staring at each other, for several seconds.

"Grace!" Mai finally exclaimed, a huge grin exploding on her face. She dropped her books and grabbed Grace in a tight hug. "I *knew* you'd apologize. I accept!"

Grace returned the hug, her mouth hanging open with the unspoken apology still inside. Without another word, they were off to school as if nothing had happened.

Pedalling slowly, Grace filled Mai in on the recent happenings. Her animated monologue was often interrupted by Mai's continuous stream of *No Way! He did what?! You didn't!*

When Grace got to the part about Fred's strange phone call, Mai chipped in. "I don't know what he's talking about either. I didn't see him yesterday. I had band

recital all day then my parents took me out to dinner."
She shrugged. "So he had a whole day unsupervised.
Who knows what nutty conspiracy theories he's cooked
up without us."

"Seriously." Grace nodded. "We've got to find out what
he's been up to."

They didn't get their chance until gym class later that
morning.

"Uh-oh," Grace and Mai moaned as they entered the
gym. Loopy Longmire, their gym teacher, was nowhere
in sight, but there was a smoky haze hovering near the
ceiling. Not incense again!

Fred beckoned them over. "There you are! You missed
all the excitement. Leroy Weller was complaining about
the stink from the incense and then puked all over Longmire's pink leotard. She cancelled gym class and hauled
him off to the nurse's office. So we have an entire double
period free, and then lunch."

"Woohoo!" Grace exclaimed. "Let's go to Black Hole.
We've got lots to talk about!"

*   *   *

"Have I got news for you!" Fred flopped down at the table in Black Hole and grabbed a chocolate cake from his
pack. "I was working one of my informants, Mr. Pulzifer—
you know, the security guard/janitor guy? It was tough,
but I kept tailing him, looking for an angle—something
I could use to muscle him." Fred paused to leisurely un-
wrap his treat.

"And...?" Mai prompted.

"I'm getting to the good part. So, my detective work
finally paid off. I followed him down to the boiler room
yesterday. He was there to sneak a puff on one of those
stinky cigars. So I tiptoed up behind him and caught him
in the act! I said to him, 'Gee, Mr. Pulzifer, isn't it against

the rules to smoke on school grounds?' Well, he knew I had him, so he coughed up what I was looking for."

Mai and Grace exchanged eye rolls at the spy talk and glared at Fred, waiting for the intel. Fred seemed to be enjoying himself and was in no hurry to relinquish being the centre of attention.

"Spill it!" Grace finally said.

Fred popped the rest of his cake into his mouth and linked his hands behind his head, grinning at Mai and Grace as he chewed.

"Fred!" Mai said.

"Okay, okay!" he yelped. "Pulzifer told me that they've been having trouble with the security cameras at school for months. And get this...you know the one in the hallway where Grace's locker is? It isn't even working. It's *disconnected*!"

"Disconnected?" Mai said. "Since when?"

"For the last month!"

"A month? But that means...wait...what *does* that mean?" Grace asked, confused. "You saw the video. We all did."

"It means," Fred said with relish, "the video was a fake!"

Chapter
18

"A FAKE? BUT WHY?" GRACE ASKED. HER VOICE WAS SHAKING. *There must be some explanation,* she thought to herself.

"Maybe Jeeter figured that it would make us like him or something," said Mai, sounding disappointed. "You know, because it made him the hero. I guess it was too good to be true."

"How did he do it?" Grace asked.

"It wouldn't be hard, Grace," Fred said. "He probably just used his own camera and then uploaded the video to his computer."

"But if he made the video, then the envelope with Stanley's name on it and the note from my dad's office must be fake, too!" Grace exclaimed.

"Note?" asked Fred, a confused look on his face. "What note?"

As Grace explained, Fred's face turned red. "He was in your house?" he spat. "When I was talking to you?"

"Don't forget that he saved my life too," Grace added. "If he was just some evil bad guy, he wouldn't have done that."

"But Jeeter *is* the bad guy," declared Fred. "It's a no-brainer. We have to find out how deep this rabbit hole goes."

"It seems like Jeeter's fixated on Rick Stanley," Mai said. "There's got to be an explanation for that."

"I think we should stake out Jeeter's place," Fred suggested. "He's in this right up to his six-pack abs and buzz-cut hair, and we need to find out why!"

"It would have to be dark, for cover," Grace said. "But there's no way I can get out of curfew. You two will have to do it."

"Too bad you can't come, Grace. But...does this mean *I'm* in charge of the mission?" Fred asked. He leapt to his feet and started to pace back and forth, fingers tapping on his chin. "Okay," he continued, "first thing we'll need to do is—"

"If you think for one second I'm going to take orders from you, your brain damage is even worse than I thought!" Mai said. "There's no way in this solar system, this galaxy, this entire *universe*—"

"Can't you two get along for five minutes?" Grace grumbled. "I can just see it now: Jeeter's whole neighbourhood will be standing there watching you two fight and you won't even know it! They'll probably have popcorn for the show. You've gotta stay undercover! Remember what that means?"

"Sorry, Grace," Mai said.

"Fine," Fred scowled. "Take all the fun out of it." He sulked for twelve seconds exactly before he was back in planning mode, making suggestions for camouflage.

They sketched out Jeeter's yard and worked out Mai and Fred's positions. Finally, Grace declared that they were as ready as they'd ever be.

*   *   *

After lunch, Grace, Mai, and Fred returned to school. They were walking down the hall discussing their plans when they rounded a corner and ran smack into Jeeter.

"Hey, just the spies I was looking for," Jeeter said, smiling. "What are you guys up to?"

Mouths hanging open, Grace, Mai, and Fred stared at him like he was a giant ogre about to chop them up for stew. Grace wanted to scratch his eyes out. *Liar,* she thought.

"What's wrong?" Jeeter asked. His smile faded and he looked behind him as if to see if the terrified reception was for someone else.

"Well, for starters—" Fred growled, stepping forward.

"Nothing!" Grace grabbed Fred's sleeve and hauled him backward. "We're just talking about, um, maybe doing a stakeout of Stanley's house this weekend."

"Great idea," Jeeter said. His eyes drifted to Mai's still-frozen face. "Are you sure there's nothing wrong?"

"Well, actually," said Grace, "Fred's walkie-talkie isn't, um, working. Could he borrow yours 'til the weekend? You don't need it, do you?"

"I guess not," Jeeter said. "What's he need it for?"

"We have to work on a school thing, and we'll probably be up late. Mom won't let me use the phone past nine."

"All right," he said reluctantly. He took his walkie-talkie from his pack and handed it to Fred.

"Well, we've got class," Grace said. She started inching away from Jeeter, dragging the still-gaping Mai with her. "We'll see you tomorrow to plan the weekend."

Grace, Mai, and Fred continued down the corridor. Grace looked back over her shoulder just as they were about to turn a corner.

Jeeter was still standing in the same spot, staring at her.

Grace gasped. She raised her hand in a quick wave and scurried around the corner.

"Good thinking, Grace, getting me a walkie-talkie," Fred said when they were out of earshot. "But mine's probably at home. I would have found it eventually."

"It wasn't for you," Mai replied, finally coming back to life. "She didn't want Jeeter listening to us over the airwaves. Right, Grace?"

Grace nodded a silent confirmation.

"Oh, good detective work." Fred smiled his approval. "So the stakeout is this weekend? Great! That'll give me time to survey the area. You know, pick out the most strategic observation posts."

Grace shook her head. "No. You've gotta go tonight!"

Chapter 19

"TONIGHT?" FRED SQUEAKED. "BUT I'M NOT READY!"

"Geez, Fred, get a grip!" Mai said. "We can handle it, Grace. No problem."

"Good," Grace said as they walked down the nearly empty hallway.

"Shoot, I'm going to be late!" Fred said suddenly, looking at his watch. "See you!" He rushed off to class.

"Come on, Mai," Grace said, opening the door to the library. "I want to check something out on the computer." They had a free period and didn't have to be in class until later.

Grace raced to the back of the room, claiming the one and only computer. She opened the web browser and typed the name *Sandstar* into the search box.

"What's Sandstar?" Mai asked, pulling a chair up beside her. "It sounds familiar."

"When I searched Dad's office, there was a ton of stuff about Sandstar," Grace replied. "That's the company that got the tar ponds cleanup project. I want to check it out, just in case it means something."

A long list of hits popped up in the search engine. Grace clicked on the first one. "Wow, look at this," she said. "The Sandstar contract is worth four hundred million dollars!"

"Hey, now I know why that name sounds familiar!" Mai's eyes glimmered with recognition. "I saw something about them when I was researching our project for Mr. Grange's class. I remember reading that it was one of the costliest environmental projects ever undertaken. But I was mainly researching the history of the contamination—I hadn't done much on the cleanup part."

"Hmm," Grace mused, clicking on another internet link. "Look at this one. It's an environmental site. They don't think the method Sandstar is using will work. That's what Dad had in his notes, too. He said an incinerator wouldn't work 'cause there's too much waste to get rid of."

"Try another one," Mai said.

They scanned the list. "Ooh, that's Sandstar's website," Mai said, pointing at a link. "Try that."

Grace clicked on the link and scanned the news section of the site. "It looks like they started the cleanup six months ago and it's on schedule. Look at all these articles—apparently they're meeting all their deadlines and the government is happy with the progress." Grace's hopes plummeted again. Another dead end.

She was about to log off when, on a whim, she searched for the Cape Breton newspaper site. When it popped up, she clicked on the obituaries and entered Beatrice Stanley, the name of Rick Stanley's great-aunt, in the search box. Nothing came up. She deleted the last name and just searched for Beatrice. Still nothing. Had he been lying about where he got the money for his car? But so what if he did? There was probably nothing wrong with the guy anyways. Jeeter was the suspect now.

*   *   *

Coasting into her driveway after school, Grace stopped short at the sight of her mom's car. *Darn.* She was supposed to be working.

"What are you doing home?" Grace asked as she walked through the back door into the kitchen. Her mom was sitting at the table, filing her nails.

"I switched shifts with Eleanor," she explained. "I wanted to spend a little time with you."

"Oh." *Ugh, gushy-gooey Mom front and centre.*

Grace's mom frowned. "How about a little enthusiasm?"

"Sorry, Mom." Grace did her best to seem happy. "Sounds fun! What do you want to do?"

"Let's do some baking," her mom replied. "I thought we'd make some squares for the community fundraiser."

"Great!" Grace said, faking a smile.

It took hours to make four different kinds of squares. Who'd want to eat them anyways? Grace wondered. She was sure her mom had mixed up the salt and baking powder measurements, but she knew better than to say anything.

"There!" her mom smiled, putting the last piece of cherry on a square. "Who says we don't make a good team?"

Grace looked up at the clock. Seven-thirty. It was getting closer and closer to night time—and spy time.

"Grace," her mom said, wiping her hand on a dish-towel. "I talked to Dr. Solomon today."

Whoa! Grace hadn't expected that. "Dr. Solomon? Why'd you do that?"

"I was concerned after our talk last night so I called him," she answered. "He wants to see you."

Grace could feel her face getting hot. "Well, *I* don't want to see *him*. I'm fine!"

"No, Grace, I don't think you are fine," her mom replied. "You talked last night as if you're trying to be some kind of detective, investigating what happened to your dad—like that's going to change anything. It's called avoidance, Grace. Believe me, I know."

"Mom—"

"Let me finish, honey. It was a terrible accident, but it happened and there's nothing we can do about it. It won't bring him back." She reached over and cupped Grace's face gently. "I worry about you. You're all I have."

Great! Now her mother thought she was having a breakdown or something.

"Come on. I have a surprise for you." She grasped Grace's hand and tugged her gently up the stairs to the master bedroom. She went to the closet and pulled down the same box Grace had seen her with the other night. She put it on the bed and patted the mattress for Grace to sit beside her.

"These are the pictures of your last fossil-hunting trip," she said. Her voice sounded shaky. "The photo shop called after your dad....Anyway, it took me a long time before I could go get them."

They spread the pictures out over the bed. Seeing her dad's smiling face—his big grin and twinkling eyes—was shocking to Grace. She picked up a picture of her and her dad together. Both of them were covered in dirt. She was waving her rock hammer over her head and her dad was holding a fossil of a calamite leaf. She remembered how he had taken forever to balance the camera on the rock ledge and set the automatic timer for that photo.

"I got that camera for your dad so I could at least see what you were both so crazy about," her mother said. "I should have gone with you two once in a while." She held up another picture of them. "You guys look like you were having a wonderful time."

"We were," Grace said, staring at their glowing faces. "You know, Mom, it's not that we didn't want you to come..." Grace looked up at her mother's sombre face. "We just didn't think you wanted to."

"I know," her mom said. "I just knew you guys were so in love with it all. I didn't want to interfere with you two, my dynamic duo."

I love you, Mom, Grace thought. She knew she should say it, but she couldn't form the words out loud. Instead, to her shock, something else popped out of her mouth. "If you think I should see Dr. Solomon, I will."

"Really?" Her mother looked relieved. "That's wonderful, honey. You know, maybe I'm too hard on you. It's been such a difficult time. How about if we cancel grounding for the weekend? A trial run. Stay out of trouble and we'll talk about getting rid of it altogether."

Grace leapt up and grabbed her mother in a stranglehold. "Thank you, thank you, thank you!" she squealed, raining kisses on her mother's cheeks.

"Okay, that's enough," her mother chuckled, gently pushing her away. "We can talk about this later. I may have to go out tonight for a manicure client. She doesn't get off work until nine-thirty. Either that or she'll come here." She glanced at her watch. "My goodness, it's almost eight-thirty!" She stood up and wiped her face. "You take the pictures, honey, I got them for you."

Grace gathered up the photos in her arms and walked back to her room. She put them down on her desk and peered out the window into the fading daylight. It was cloudy.

It was going to be a perfect night for spying.

Chapter
20

"COME IN, GRACE," CAME FRED'S VOICE THROUGH THE WALKIE-talkie. "Code alpha two. I repeat, code alpha two."

"Fred, will you knock off the weird codes?!" Grace replied. "I don't know what you're saying."

"Aw, fine, if you want to be boring!" Fred griped. "I'm in position in an oak tree facing Jeeter's driveway."

"You're in a *tree*? Off the *ground*?" Grace asked, visions of a cracked skull and broken limbs flashing in her mind.

"Ha, ha, very funny."

"Hey guys, lock your transmit buttons to on," Grace said. "That way I'll be able to hear everything." *It's lucky Mom went out for her manicure appointment, after all—otherwise she'd have been able to hear this noise all over the house!* Grace thought to herself.

"Mai checking in," came Mai's voice. "I'm on the opposite side of Jeeter's house and have a clear view of the kitchen and living room through—"

"*Shhhh*," Fred hushed suddenly. "Someone's coming!"

"Who is it?" Mai whispered. "I can't see you from here."

"Hold on, they're pulling into the driveway," Fred replied.

The airwaves were silent for a minute.

"Fred?" Grace finally said. "What's happening?" She held her breath as she heard Fred muttering and moving around.

"Oh, never mind," he said finally. "False alarm."

Grace shrugged her shoulders up and down, trying to get rid of the tension. As she listened to Mai and Fred whisper back and forth she was also watching Stuckless through the bedroom window. She was curious what her other suspect was up to.

Stuckless was in the basement again, and he appeared to be fiddling with the same device she'd seen him with last night. There was no feedback coming in on her walkie-talkie. Maybe he was listening instead.

"Fred, come in," she said, peering intently through her binoculars at the same time. Yes, there it was! Stuckless had leaned forward the moment she'd spoken.

"I think we definitely have to watch Stuckless more closely," she continued, her eyes glued to the binoculars.

Bingo! Stuckless's head whipped around and he looked right up at her window! Her theory was bang on. He was listening to something, all right—*her*!

"Grace, what are you talking about?" Mai said.

"Never mind," she said. No sense getting into it right now. Mai and Fred had enough to worry about. She must have freaked Stuckless out anyway. His basement light went out and a minute later the light was on upstairs.

This sure explained a lot, like how Stuckless kept showing up where they were all the time. She thought back to their trip to Point Aconi—they had been using their walkie-talkies the whole time. No wonder he had known where they were.

But why would Stuckless be interested in their conversations? Or in anything they did? They were only kids. *Maybe Dad had been suspicious of him,* Grace thought. *It must have something to do with the strip mines.*

Grace put her binoculars back in her pack. Her dad's bag was sitting beside it. She flipped it open, pulling out the fossil tucked in the front pouch. It was one of the best specimens of a cyclopteris leaf she'd ever seen. She wished she'd been with him when he'd found it. They had found a great one at the PA2, too, Grace remembered. It had been a cold day, and they'd packed thermoses full of hot chocolate...

"Someone's pulling into the driveway!" Fred's voice blared over the walkie-talkie and brought Grace back to reality with a jolt.

"Who is it?" she asked. "Another false alarm?"

"Nope. It's the real deal this time. A man in a suit is getting out of the car. He must be Jeeter's dad. Now he's walking toward the house. It looks like he's coming home from work—he's carrying a bunch of files or papers or something. I can almost make out one of the labels on the files—it starts with an S." Fred's voice was getting louder by the second—Grace could hear his excitement building up. "Sydney Mines—"

"Shhh," Mai warned. "He'll hear you."

"Sorry," Fred said, lowering his voice. "He's turning toward. Wait for it...no, I don't believe it!"

"What is it?" Grace said, craning forward as if trying to see it for herself. She clutched her walkie-talkie tightly in her hands. *"Fred!* What is it?"

"Uh-oh," Fred groaned.

"Hey you! What are you doing in that tree?" a male voice demanded. "Come down from there immediately!"

"Whooo? Meeee?" came Fred's voice.

"Don't get smart, young man. Do you see anyone else up there in that tree with you?" The man's voice was loud—and angry.

Grace could hear everything clearly, but she couldn't do anything for Fred. She felt so helpless.

Suddenly another voice joined in. "It's okay, Roger."

Was that Jeeter's voice?

"Stay out of this, Marcus. I'll handle it. This hoodlum was probably casing out our house to rob us. I'm calling the police!"

"No he wasn't. I know him. We were just goofing around."

"Goofing around? I don't have time for your childish games, Marcus. Get your *friend* out of our tree and say goodnight. And don't forget you have to call you mother tonight."

"Yes, sir," Jeeter mumbled.

Grace heard Jeeter's father mumble something else, but she couldn't make it out. He must have been out of range.

"C'mon, Sherlock, try to get down without breaking your neck," Jeeter said. "Give me your arm before you kill yourself."

"I don't need your help!" Fred said. "And why is your dad calling you Marcus?"

"Marcus, say goodnight!" his father bellowed.

"I gotta go, Freddo. But we'll talk later about why *I'm* being spied on!" Jeeter said. "Goodnight, Grace," he added.

Back in her room, her ear pressed to her walkie-talkie, Grace gasped. Her head was spinning. What was going on? Call his *mother*? She was dead. Did he have a stepmother? No, he'd said it was just him and his dad. And why did his dad call him Marcus?

Tears welled in Grace's eyes. Was everything Jeeter had told her a lie?

"Grace, did you hear all that?" Fred said. "Grace, are you there?"

"What? Yes, I'm here," Grace sniffed.

"You're not going to believe this…" Fred said. "Jeeter's dad had an armful of files from the Sydney Mines Fossil Museum!"

Chapter
21

"I DON'T UNDERSTAND," GRACE SAID. "WHY WOULD JEETER'S DAD have anything to do with the museum? How does he even know about it?"

"I don't know," Fred said.

"But Jeeter said his dad worked with Environment Canada!" Grace cried.

"Calm down, Grace," Mai's voice soothed. "Do you want us to come over?"

Grace peered out the window. Her mom's car was still gone. "Okay," she murmured. She closed her eyes and took a deep breath to slow her racing heart. She was still clutching her dad's fossil.

CRASH!

Suddenly a huge roar filled her ears as rain erupted from the skies in torrents. It was coming down so hard that the droplets bounced off the pavement. Spikes of lightning exploded in the sky like fireworks. *Rain like this means more sinkholes*, Grace thought as she tucked the fossil in her pocket and went downstairs to wait for Mai and Fred.

*   *   *

Grace, Mai, and Fred sat around the kitchen table in silence. Grace was lost in her thoughts and Fred's attempts at jokes had lamely petered off when he hadn't even received so much as an eyelid twitch in response.

Mai and Fred had been drenched and shivering when they'd arrived. Grace had found two jumbo beach towels and they'd wrapped themselves up. Mai had made hot chocolate.

"Come on, Grace," Mai coaxed, pushing the steaming mug closer to her. "Have some. I put mini marshmallows in there."

Grace stared ahead blankly. "All that talk about how he understood what I was going through with my dad because he'd lost his mother—it was all lies! He probably just said that stuff to get close to me. What a creep! And what's his dad doing at the museum, anyways?"

"I don't know, Grace." Mai reached over and hugged her. "But we'll find out. Don't worry."

Fred slurped his hot chocolate. "Maybe there's something going on at the fossil museum. Maybe Jeeter's dad wants to be famous, like that guy who found the dinosaur in the Alberta Badlands. And Jeeter is helping him!"

"Well, there's definitely *something* weird going on! He had all those mining maps in the basement, remember?" Grace said. "They were the same kind my dad has." She absentmindedly pulled her dad's fossil from her pocket and twirled it around in her fingers.

"Nice fossil," Fred said, leaning over to get a better look.

"It was in my dad's bag when I found it at Point Aconi the other day," said Grace.

"Wait a minute!" Fred cried, banging down his cup. Hot chocolate and mini marshmallows sprayed over the tabletop. "Point Aconi! I bet that's where I lost my walkie-talkie. You know, when I fell in that sinkhole."

"It's only a walkie-talkie," Grace said. "Don't worry about it. Besides, you have Jeeter's."

"Can I see your fossil, Grace?" Mai asked. She held it up to get a closer look.

Grace stared at the back of the fossil as Mai was looking at the front. "That's weird. It's been catalogued already," she said, staring at the coded label. "If it's already coded, it's supposed to be in the museum collection."

"Maybe your dad just didn't pass it in yet," Fred said, shrugging. "You don't have to give it back, do you?"

Grace didn't answer. She stared at the code. Something wasn't right.

Heart racing, Grace bolted up to her room. She ran back to the kitchen clutching her mining map. Mai was wiping up Fred's chocolate spill.

"Move your cups," Grace ordered. She spread her map out on the table. Her eyes scanned the Point Aconi area. It was just as she thought. The code didn't match any of their fossil sites!

"It's not here," she whispered. Her hands shook as they ran lightly over the map "It isn't on the map."

"What does that mean?" Fred asked, sounding confused. "That he found it somewhere else? Joggins, maybe?"

"No, I don't think so," Grace said. "Look at the code: SYD-09-PA4-01. 'SYD' means the Sydney coalfields—basically, that's all of Cape Breton—'09' means the year, and 'PA4' means the exact spot—the fourth sinkhole in Point Aconi. See? Look here on the map. The PA3 was the last place in Point Aconi we had marked down."

"So?" Fred said. "Maybe you missed one of the sinkholes when you copied your dad's map."

"No, don't you see?" Grace said. "This has got to be a new sinkhole. It must be where my dad was working before he disappeared. The '01' in the code means this is the first find at that site." She pointed to an area on the map between the PA3 sinkhole and the shore. "The PA4's got to be somewhere in here. We've got to find it!"

"Why?" Fred asked.

"Well, I found his field bag at the PA3," Grace replied. "If he's already been to the PA4, there could be more clues there!"

"Well, maybe," Mai said. "But that's still a lot of area. How are we going to find it?"

"Since his bag was at the PA3 sinkhole, partway down the mine tunnel, I bet the PA4 is through that same tunnel. Look, see how all the sites run in a line?" Grace connected each site with her finger. "If we follow the tunnel along that line, we'll find the PA4. I'm sure of it!"

"What do you think we'll find there?" Mai asked.

Grace looked at Mai and Fred excitedly. "There has to be something more. I just know it!"

"It could be dangerous," Fred said. "Maybe we should we go to the police."

"Who would believe a bunch of kids?" Grace said. "And what would we tell them, anyways? We have to find more evidence!"

THUD!

The sound of a car door slamming interrupted Grace's train of thought.

"Crap!" Grace whispered fiercely. "Mom's back! You've got to get out of here!" If her mom caught Mai and Fred here, she could forget about being allowed out tomorrow. That would ruin everything.

Fred jumped to his feet, knocking over the rest of his hot chocolate.

"Fred!" Mai yelped, throwing a towel over the spill.

"Sorry!"

Grace dumped the mugs in the sink, poured some dish detergent in, and turned the tap on. Water gushed out of the faucet, covering the evidence with foaming suds. "Gimme that!" She grabbed the chocolate-soaked towel from Mai and dumped it in the water.

Slam!

Oh, no! The front door. Her mom was inside!

Grace heard her mom's high heels clicking on the tile of the front entryway.

"Hurry up!" she hissed. She shoved Fred out the back door. He hopped through, still pulling on his sneaker. Mai followed quickly behind him.

Grace ran back to the sink and thrust her hands into the scalding water just as her mother came through the door from the hallway.

"It's really coming down out there," Grace's mother said as she shook her coat off and hung it on the hook by the back door. She reached up and fluffed her hair. "I'm soaked."

Grace peered out the kitchen window. The rain was coming down even harder than before. "Wow, is it ever!" she agreed. She hoped Fred and Mai got home okay.

"You're doing dishes without being asked?" Her mother looked at her strangely. "Well, isn't that nice?" She smiled and kissed Grace's forehead.

"No problem, Mom."

Her mother mumbled something about getting changed and went upstairs.

As Grace watched the rain sloshing out of the drainpipes and turning the garden into oozing mud, she had a vision of all of Sydney Mines collapsing into one giant sinkhole.

Chapter 22

"THIS IS HOPELESS!" MAI MOANED, SITTING DOWN ON A FALLEN LOG. She reached down to rub her shin and frowned at her mud-covered hiking boots. "My feet are killing me."

Grace's legs were sore too. There were puddles of water everywhere, and moving around felt like trying to walk on a wet sponge.

They had been searching for the PA3 sinkhole for ages, with no luck. It was much harder to find an exact spot than Grace had thought, even with a map. None of them had paid much attention to landmarks the first time they'd come. Who knew they'd want to find it again?

"It took us two hours to get here and we've been roaming around at least that long," Grace complained. "The day will be over and we won't have accomplished anything."

"That darn hole is around here somewhere, I know it is," Fred said, continuing ahead, his eyes glued to the ground.

Grace plunked down beside Mai and pulled out her water bottle. She took a long drink. "Maybe we should just concentrate on trying to find the new site, the PA4. It would be closer to the shore."

"Why don't we look at the map again?" Mai suggested. "Maybe it'll help."

Grace was feeling discouraged. She'd been so sure the day would be perfect, like it was meant to be or something. She'd come here, find the PA3 and PA4...

Grace grabbed the map from her pack and unfolded it. She and Mai held it between them, examining the area closely. Mai traced out the markings lightly with her finger, occasionally lifting her head to scan their surroundings. It was no use. The map couldn't help much when they were surrounded by trees.

"Let's get back to searching," Grace sighed, dejected.

"Sorry, Grace," Mai said, reaching out to touch her arm.

Grace shrugged and moved away, avoiding Mai's touch. She felt like she'd crumple into a ball and never move again if she didn't keep going. Mai looked hurt and quickly pulled her hand back.

"Aaaaaaahhhhh!!!"

They both whipped around at the same time. Fred had disappeared.

"Fred, where are you?" Mai cried, running in the direction of his scream.

"Uh, I think I found it!" came his muffled yell. They both looked down. Fred was sprawled on the ground in a sinkhole.

"Oh, there you are," said Grace. She peered down into the crater. It was so wide—how had they missed it?

"Next time, try *not* falling in the hole," Mai shouted down to Fred. "You're going to get yourself killed!" She turned to Grace. "At least that's one thing we can scratch off Jeeter's list of crimes. He didn't push Fred."

"Geez!" Fred muttered from below. "It's not like I fall on purpose!"

Grace felt the excitement well up inside her. She tied her caving rope securely to a nearby oak tree. After pulling on her caving gloves, she carefully lowered herself into the sinkhole. The descent was jerky. Chunks of earth at the edge of the hole kept breaking away, tumbling into the open space below her. Water dripped in steady streams around her from the wet ground above.

Grace's heart was hammering. Her instincts were screaming that this was a bad idea. The line jerked even more as she lowered herself another metre.

"Grace," Mai said from above, "all this rain...are you sure—?"

"It'll be okay," Grace said. She ignored the uneasiness crawling up her spine.

Grace touched down at the bottom of the hole and tilted her head back to watch Mai's descent. It started out smoothly, but halfway down the line jerked.

"Help!" Mai cried. She spun crazily in a circle, her eyes wide and frightened.

"Take it easy," Grace soothed. She grabbed the bottom of the rope to steady it.

More clumps of dirt and grass fell down from the lip of the crater. The ground up top was too wet to hold.

"Come on," Grace encouraged. The sooner Mai was on solid ground, the better.

Mai slowly descended into the sinkhole. Her hands held the rope in a death grip. When she finally touched down, she sagged against Grace. "Whew," she breathed. "That wasn't fun."

Grace gave her shoulder a quick squeeze.

"Hey, guys," Fred called, sounding excited. "Look at this!" He emerged from a nearby tunnel and handed something to Grace.

Her heart jumped. It was another fossil. Could it be another clue? She flipped it over. *Darn!* No code.

Grace retrieved her flashlight from her pack and walked into the tunnel, shining her beam on the floor. Fred and Mai followed behind her.

There were pieces of broken shale everywhere. Bending over to get a closer look, Grace could see outlines of seed ferns, cyclopteris leaves, and calamite tree bark in the shale fragments. The remnants of an entire carboniferous forest were scattered at her feet! She picked up a beautiful stigmaria fossil and carried it back to the tunnel opening to get a better look in the natural light.

"Fred, Mai," she called. "Come and see this one."

BBARRUMMBRRGG!!!

Suddenly, the sky was falling. Rocks and earth crashed down from above, blocking out the light. It was another cave-in!

Grace heard a scream. Before she could run toward the sound, pain exploded in her right arm. Instinctively, Grace crouched low and covered her head with her uninjured arm, keeping her other one close to her chest. Debris continued to fall all around her. Dust clogged the air and filled her mouth. It was getting hard to breathe.

Something hit Grace in the shoulder, knocking her off balance. As she tumbled sideways, she saw Mai and Fred collapsing under a pile of earth.

They were all going to die!

Chapter
23

"DAD," GRACE SAID. "THIS ONE'S NOT GOING TO COME OUT."

"Patience, Grace." He was crouched beside her on Battlemen's Beach. Waves from Hurricane Ivan had beaten the shore and cliffs all the previous day. Now, it was sunny and calm. Barely a ripple broke the ocean surface in the early morning sun.

Grace and her dad had been the first ones to the beach when the tide went out, excited to see what treasures the waves had wrenched from the cliffs.

Trying to keep her eagerness in check, Grace concentrated on tapping gently but firmly on the large piece of slate. The sigillaria tree bark fossil was perfect—or it would be, if only she could get it out.

Her dad reached over and adjusted her grip. "Gently, now," he cautioned. "You don't want to split the fossil."

Grace held up her hammer, defeated. "You'd better do it!"

"No, Grace. I know you can do it. Keep going."

"Like this?" Grace tapped lightly with the rock hammer.

"Exactly!" her dad cheered. "A light touch. You're doing great. You're going to be a pro before you know it!"

Grace beamed with pride.

"Grace."

She looked around. Who said that? "Dad, did you hear something?"

He smiled down at her silently.

"Grace, wake up!"

Who was doing that? She wished they would stop.

Suddenly the fossil broke free in her hands. She held it up in triumph. "I got it, Dad!"

But the sun and ocean had disappeared—her dad, too. Grace couldn't see anything. Her arm was throbbing and her mouth tasted like dirt. Someone was shaking her gently.

She slowly opened her eyes, only to squint them closed again.

"You're alive!" someone shouted, grabbing her and squeezing her.

"Ow!" she screamed. "My arm!"

"Oops, sorry."

She opened her eyes again. Fred's face was inches from hers. He had a scratch down the side of his cheek and a thin trickle of blood was snaking a path through the soot on his face. His white teeth were a shocking contrast against the coal dust as he broke into a toothy grin.

"I thought you were...that you'd—" he broke off.

"I think I'm okay," she said. "But I hurt my arm. Help me up?"

Grace reached with her uninjured arm to grasp Fred's outstretched hand.

"Where's Mai?"

He didn't answer.

Fear clutched at Grace's stomach. Something was wrong. "Fred?" she said, afraid to look away from him.

Fred grimaced. "She's okay. Sort of."

"What do you mean, 'sort of'?" She stood up gingerly and stepped over the piles of rubble to a smoother spot on the ground. She heard a sniffle and her eyes swung wildly in the direction from where it came. Her eyes finally adjusted to the dark and she saw Mai sitting curled up against the wall in a corner.

Crouching down beside her, Grace wrapped her arm around Mai's shoulders. "Shhh...it's okay," she whispered.

"Sorry, Grace," Mai mumbled, rubbing her face. "I'm not brave like you are. I'm scared."

You've got it all wrong, Mai, Grace thought. *I'm not brave at all.* She brushed the hair back from Mai's face and tucked it behind her ear. "Don't be sorry. This is my fault. I should never have asked you guys to come here." Guilt clawed the inside of Grace's stomach as she looked at her two best friends' wide and terrified eyes.

"Don't worry. We're gonna get out of here," she said, trying to sound upbeat. "How about a little help?" She pointed to her sore arm.

Mai seemed to perk up a bit as she went into nurse mode, wrapping Grace's arm in a sling from her first aid kit. As Mai cleaned Fred's cut, Grace prowled around the tunnel, looking for an exit. The opening they'd come down was totally blocked from the cave-in. She shone her light in the opposite direction. The tunnel was blocked on the other side, too, but it looked like there might be a gap at the top of the rubble.

Grimacing in pain, Grace carefully climbed the pile to see if they could get through the gap. If they were able to move some of the rocks, they might be able to squeeze through. Then they'd hopefully find the PA4 sinkhole farther down the tunnel and be able to get out that way.

Grace called for Mai and Fred to come help her move the rocks. Grace couldn't do much lifting with her arm in a sling, but she moved what rocks she could and shouted encouragement to Fred and Mai as they lifted away the heavier ones. They removed as much as they were able. But there was one big boulder in the way. It wouldn't budge—no matter how hard they tried.

"Oh, man," Fred said after they'd been working for what seemed like hours. "It's a furnace in here. I need a sugar fix." He climbed down, dug some chocolate bars from his back-pack, and passed them around. "Anyone want a drink?"

Grace grabbed a can of pop and sighed as the warm soda trickled down the back of her parched throat. It tasted wonderful.

"Mmm...." Mai sighed in between mouthfuls of her chocolate bar. "Fred, I'll never tease you about your choco stash again." She looked down at her sticky hand. Grace waited for the handy wipe to come out. Instead, Mai shrugged and continued eating.

Grace leaned against the wall and stared up at the mound of rocks. They had been working for a long time and it had barely made a difference. Not with that monster boulder still on top, anyway. And what if they did get through? What if the rest of the tunnel was blocked too? They could be stuck here forever. Shuddering, she wondered if someone would be examining her fossil bones in this very spot in a hundred million years.

Grace looked over at Fred and Mai. They were huddled together, whispering. A lump swelled in her throat. They had always come when she'd called, did whatever she'd said. She'd always had to be the boss. Some friend she was. She'd really done it this time.

Kchhhhh!!!!

"Come in, Grace," her walkie-talkie squawked suddenly. "Grace, Mai, Fred! Where are you guys?"

Grace scrambled to her pack. "Jeeter, is that you?"

"Yeah," he replied. "Where are you?"

"We're trapped. There was a cave-in. We're in big trouble here. Where are you?" Grace sputtered into her walkie-talkie.

"I'm at another sinkhole out here," he said. "I thought it was the same one as before, but I think I missed it and went too far."

"It must be the PA4!" Grace cried. "I think it's part of this same tunnel. Can you get in? Is it clear?"

"I'm in it already," he said.

"Can you get to us?" she asked. Mai and Fred had jumped up and they all huddled around Grace's walkie-talkie.

"I'll try," he said. "Hold tight."

Grace closed her eyes and prayed. *Please, please, please, let him find us.*

"Grace?" Fred whispered.

"What?"

"I have Jeeter's walkie-talkie, remember? Where did he get another one?"

Weird, Grace thought. *More secrets.*

"What difference does it make, as long as he gets us out of here?" Mai said.

"She's right," Grace said. "Now's not the time for questions."

They huddled together in the small circle of the flashlight. Dust swirled and curled in the beam like black smoke from a pipe. The minutes ticked by.

"Hey," Jeeter called, finally.

Grace looked down at her walkie-talkie. The sound hadn't come from there—he was on the other side of the blockage!

"Are you guys all right?" he called again. "I'm gonna try and push through the rocks. Stay back."

They could hear Jeeter grunting as he pushed against the large boulder at the top of the pile. Grace watched in anticipation.

Nothing happened.

Jeeter kept trying, but only a few small rocks tumbled down. They could hear his muffled curses and groans as he pushed.

It wasn't working.

"Jeeter, stop," Grace finally said. "It's no use!"

"It's this big honker on top," Jeeter muttered. "If I could just budge it a bit, I think it would roll right down."

Staring up at the boulder, Grace tried to think. She had watched her dad around rocks her whole life. Sometimes at the shore, he would wedge a piece of driftwood under a heavy rock to move it out of the way. Could that work?

"Fred, see if there's any wood around," she ordered. "Maybe from an old rafter or something."

"Wood?" he asked with a hint at his old joking self. "We can't have a bonfire now! I don't have marshmallows for s'mores."

"Very funny," Mai said. She turned to Grace. "There are some old planks stacked on the side here." She pointed to the wall. "Will one of these work?"

"It might," Grace said hopefully.

Grace instructed Fred and Mai where to wedge the plank, hoping she remembered it right. The top of the board was almost touching the ceiling. They were going to have to pull down on it instead of pushing from above like her dad normally did. "Okay, we'll have to work together," she told Fred and Mai. "Jeeter, you push on the boulder from your side."

"I hope the wood doesn't crack," Mai said. "It's so old..."

"Keep your fingers crossed!" Fred said.

They got in position. "Ready!" Grace called out. "One, two, three, go!" She, Fred, and Mai pulled on the plank with all their might while Jeeter pushed from behind.

Grace felt the boulder move. *It was working!* She put all her weight into pulling the plank down, ignoring the burst of pain in her arm.

Suddenly the boulder dislodged from its place and started rolling toward them.

"Out of the way!" Grace cried.

Chapter
24

GRACE, MAI, AND FRED JUMPED OUT OF THE BOULDER'S PATH JUST in time. It rumbled past them and crashed to the ground below.

"Let's get out of here!" Fred cried as he scrambled down the rock pile and returned with their packs. The three of them wiggled through the opening as fast as they could.

Jeeter helped them down the other side and they raced toward the PA4.

Grace's arm was throbbing, but it didn't matter. She was focused on getting out of the tunnel. No one wanted to get caught in another cave-in.

Finally, a faint glow of light appeared ahead of them. Grace saw Jeeter's rope hanging down from the side of the opening. They'd made it to the PA4!

"Woohoo!" Fred cried. "We're safe!"

"I can't believe we made it," Mai said, tilting her head up. "It's so nice to see the sky again."

Now that they were out of immediate danger, anger began boiling in Grace's stomach. Yes, Jeeter had saved them. But it didn't matter to her right then. She whirled around to confront him. "You lied to me!" she blurted out. She could hear a tremor in her voice.

"I didn't have any choice," Jeeter said.

"What do you mean?" she spat.

"Grace, please! Can't we talk about this later?" He touched her hand. "You can trust me."

"Trust you?" she said, pulling her hand away. "I told you everything! All I got back was lies!"

"I just saved your life."

"Why?" she whispered. "Why did you lie?"

"I had to."

"What does that even mean?" Grace shook her head. "All those lies about Stanley. The faked video, the note... why would you do all that? This is my life! Was it all some kind of sick game to you?"

"Game? No!" Jeeter looked into her eyes. "Grace, I—"

"Shhh," Mai hushed suddenly. "Do you hear that?" She pointed above them.

Everyone stepped back into the cloak of darkness.

"Flashlights!" Mai whispered. They all clicked off their lights.

A shadow fell across the opening.

"Dad, there's a rope here. Do you think it's those kids?"

"I wouldn't doubt it!" Stuckless's voice was loud and clear. "They're up to something. Let's go back to the truck and get some gear. We'll have to go down there!"

A beam of light swung back and forth in the sinkhole.

Grace, Mai, Fred, and Jeeter receded further into the dark.

Jeeter leaned over and spoke quietly in Grace's ear. "You and Mai stay here. We'll see if there's another way out." He motioned for Fred to follow him. The two of them disappeared into the darkness of the tunnel like ghosts.

"We should go with them, shouldn't we?" Mai asked softly.

"They'll come back if they find anything," Grace murmured. "Come over this way, farther from the opening." They couldn't hear Stuckless, but he could have pretended to leave and might still be above them.

Grace paced slowly back and forth through the tunnel, away from the opening. This was one of the last spots her dad might have been. She shone her flashlight back and forth across the ground in front of her as she paced, looking for any sort of clue that would tie her dad to this place.

Out of the corner of her eye, Grace noticed something in the dirt a metre or so away. She bent down to take a closer look. There were strange markings on the ground— a row of circle marks imprinted in the dust. "Mai, come see this," she called quietly. "Isn't it weird?"

"That *is* weird," Mai agreed as she bent down to look.

Grace shone her beam around, looking for clues as to what could have made the circles. "Hey!" she said. "There are more marks over here—maybe from a wheelbarrow or something—and footprints, too."

"Why would there be a wheelbarrow down here?" Mai asked.

Grace walked along the edge of the wall. Her foot banged into something and she stumbled forward, her fingers brushing against some sort of fabric. She felt for the edge of the cloth and pulled. Underneath it were black barrels— a whole row of them. Grace shone her light on one. There was something painted in bright yellow on its side:

DANGER
TOXIC WASTE
SANDSTAR
ENVIRONMENTAL
CORPORATION

Sandstar? That was the company that had won the tar ponds project. What was going on here?

"What's that?" Mai asked, coming up beside her.

"Don't touch that!" Grace warned.

"Oh my gosh—it's toxic waste!"

"I think it's from the tar ponds," Grace said, backing away. Her thoughts flashed to the sites she'd visited on the internet. The cleanup using the incinerator. Sandstar's claims that they were on schedule. She remembered her dad's doubts that it could handle all the waste. She flashed her beam along the rows of toxic waste in the abandoned tunnel. Her dad and the environmentalists had been right all along! Sandstar must be secretly dumping the waste the incinerator couldn't handle! "Mai, we have to get out of here!"

"What's wrong?"

"Sandstar—that's the company that has the contract for the tar ponds cleanup," Grace said.

"What do you mean?"

"Don't you see?" Grace said, tilting her injured arm toward the barrels. "They're dumping toxic waste in the tunnels! I bet that's why Stuckless was following us. He must be involved somehow!"

Mai swung her light across the floor. "But look at these circle marks on the ground. They're the same size as those barrels. It looks like there used to be a lot more toxic waste here."

Grace frowned. "Why would they go to all the trouble to hide the barrels here just to take them out again?" She moved slowly along the row to examine the barrels more closely.

A bit farther down the line, Grace noticed something sticking out from between two of them. She bent down and tugged it loose. When she saw what it was, she gasped and collapsed to the floor.

"What is it?" Mai peered over her shoulder.

"My dad's hat," Grace choked. "He was wearing it the morning he disappeared." It felt like she was in a trance. "That means he was here that day." She held the hat gently in her hand and traced the embroidered letters on the front: D-A-L. She couldn't believe what she was seeing.

The hat had a tear on one side and there were dark marks splattered across the normally white material. Grace couldn't breathe. She stood up, slowly made her way to the sinkhole opening, and held the hat up under the light. "There are weird stains on the brim," she said. "And they're not coal dust—they're kind of reddish."

"Oh my gosh," Mai said, touching her arm. "Is that blood?"

"Blood?" Grace closed her eyes. She felt like she was going to throw up.

"It s-s-sure looks like it," Mai stuttered.

"It can't be," Grace mumbled, clutching the hat protectively to her chest. But if Sandstar was dumping toxic waste and her dad had found out...

She opened her eyes slowly and stared at the stains. *Of course* it was blood. Grace sank to the ground. She was finished running away from the truth. The part of her that had always thought that maybe he was alive felt like it was shrivelling up.

It was over.

"We found a way out!" Jeeter said, appearing from around the corner. "There's another tunnel off this one that goes right to the ocean."

Neither Grace nor Mai moved.

"What's the matter?" Jeeter asked. "I said we found a way out. Come on!"

"It's her dad," Mai said. She was tugging her hair again. "I think Grace is in shock or something. She found his hat!"

Jeeter looked startled as his glance fell to the blood-stained hat. "What happened?" he asked.

Mai shone her flashlight on the toxic waste barrels. "Her dad must have found the guys who were dumping this toxic waste in the tunnels," she said in a hushed voice.

"Oh, no," Jeeter said. His voice sounded hollow.

"I don't know what to do," Mai said. "I'm not sure Grace can even hear us!"

"Well, we can't stay here," Jeeter said. "Stuckless is coming. It's not safe. C'mon, Grace. Get up."

Grace felt like a rag doll. Her brain didn't seem to be connected to her arms and legs. She watched as if from far away as Jeeter pulled frantically on her sleeve. She figured she should get up. He wanted her to.

"*Grace*, what's the matter with you?" Jeeter said, tugging harder on her sleeve. "Didn't you hear me? We have to go!"

Mai knelt down beside Grace and brushed the hair from her eyes. "We have to go," she spoke softly in her ear. "Grace? Can you hear me?"

Grace leaned forward and closed her eyes, touching her forehead against Mai's. "I don't know what to do," she sobbed. She could feel warm tears on her face.

"We'll figure this out," Mai said, taking her hand. "I promise."

Grace looked into Mai's concerned eyes. She was such a good friend. But what could she do? The unthinkable had already happened.

"What's taking you guys so long?" Fred panted, racing into view.

Mai pulled Grace to her feet and held her hand tightly as she led her away. Just before they turned the corner, Grace looked back, squinting to see the spot where she'd found her dad's hat—the place where he had to have been. But there was only darkness.

Chapter 25

THEY ROUNDED A TURN INTO THE LIGHT AND GRACE SQUINTED against the glare. She could smell the ocean.

"C'mon, hurry!" Fred shouted back to them. He was teetering on a big boulder at the edge of the water. There was only a metre or so between the cliff and the rising tide.

The beach was littered with mounds of dried kelp, and its rotting, salty smell mingled with the damp sea air. Rain was exploding from the thunderheads above. Stinging needles of water pelted Grace's face and arms as she emerged onto the beach. The pain on the outside seemed to dull some of the pain inside and she tilted her face upward, welcoming more.

"Where are we, anyway?" Mai asked. She looked back and forth along the shore. "Grace?"

"What?"

"Do you know this place? It's not Battlemen's Beach, that's for sure!" Mai's voice rose.

Grace shook her head. *What does it matter now?* she thought.

Mai's fingers closed gently around Grace's wrist. "It's important!" she said firmly.

Grace sighed. "Well, we were at the PA4, which is pretty much under the Point Aconi lighthouse." She glanced above them to the cliffs. "Look, you can see the tip of it up there."

Grace stepped onto a flat boulder at the edge of the waves. She leaned as far forward as she dared. "There!" she said, pointing. "I can see the very tip of Little Table Island. The rest of it is hidden by the point."

"So we're on the opposite side of the point, then?" Fred asked. "We've never been here before."

Grace pulled the map out of her dad's field bag. She spread it out on the rocky beach. Point Aconi stretched like a long finger into the ocean. She traced along the right side of the point with her finger. "That's Battlemen's Beach." She pointed to a small sliver off the point. "And this is Little Table Island."

"Oh," Mai said, crouching down beside Grace. "So we're here, then?" She touched the left side of the long finger on the map.

"We have to be," Grace nodded.

"Uh, guys?" Fred broke in. "The tide's almost in. And it doesn't look like we can get back to Battlemen's Beach from here—the water's already risen all the way up to the cliffs that way. We're gonna get trapped here if we don't start moving!"

Grace looked up at the towering cliff beside them. *Always stay as far away from the rock face as it is high.* Her dad's words echoed in her head. *But his warning isn't much good to us now,* she thought as she watched the small waves from the incoming tide curl around her feet. She was close enough to touch the crumbling slate of the cliff face.

There was nowhere to go. If there were a rock slide, they'd be buried.

"Grace?" Mai said. "What are we going to do? The water...it's everywhere." Her voice was high and scratchy.

"Have you ever been on this side of the point?" Jeeter asked. "Where would we end up if we go down that way?" He pointed off in the other direction, away from Battlemen's Beach.

"I don't know," Grace said. "My dad and I never came this far before. I always wanted to come around the point by boat and see this side of the beach from the water." She remembered pleading with her dad to come over here. He'd promised to take her one day. "But we never did..." she trailed off.

"Well, what choice do we have?" Mai squeaked, flinging dripping strands of hair away from her face. "We can't go back into the tunnel, not with the chance of another cave-in!"

"Yeah, pancake city!" Fred said, slapping his two hands together. "Besides, that Stuckless guy is coming back for us, remember?"

Grace shuddered.

"Guys?" Fred said. "Whatever we're doing, we'd better do it, like, *pronto.*"

The water had now risen past Fred's ankles. Their tiny scrap of shore was disappearing fast.

For a second Grace felt like just leaning against the cliff and waiting for the water to come and take her away. It would be so easy.

"Come on," Jeeter said. He scurried over the huge boulders on the beach, not looking back.

Fred started to follow behind Jeeter, but his foot slipped on the wet surface of a boulder and he banged his knee against the stone. "Ouch!" He turned back toward Grace and Mai, frowning and rubbing his shin.

"Are you okay?" Mai asked.

"Yeah, of course," Fred bluffed. "I'm fine."

He jumped back up on the boulder and held his hand out to help Mai.

"Thanks, Fred," she said as she grabbed his hand.

Fred's face shone as he pulled Mai up beside him. He didn't let go of her as they continued over the rocks.

Grace gazed longingly at the approaching waves and sighed. Sluggishly, she picked up the rear. Watching everyone's back was a different view, she mused. She was used to being the leader. As she followed, she overheard Mai filling Fred in about the toxic waste and finding her dad's hat.

The rain had finally stopped, but the rocks were still slick and dangerous. Wet clumps of seaweed hid gaps between the boulders, and more than one trapped foot had to be yanked free as they clambered over the uneven shore. Blood oozed from the nicks and scratches they obtained from grasping at the sharp barnacles that encrusted most of the rock surfaces. Gulls screamed overhead. It was like they were in a hostile alien world.

Grace felt as if she'd forgotten everything she'd ever known. She was lost in a daze. Only having one arm to balance made it even tougher, but she refused all offers of help. It was Mai who'd finally suggested using their caving gloves to protect their hands from the barnacles. Grace couldn't believe that she hadn't thought of that.

After a torturous half hour, Grace, Mai, Fred, and Jeeter finally hit a clearing with a few flat boulders. They collapsed to rest and examine their injuries.

"Be careful, these are the last of the bandages," Mai warned. "Fred! You have to clean the wound first!" She tossed him the disinfectant.

"Me?" he said. "Aren't you going to do it?"

"Oh, for goodness sake," she griped. But she was smiling as she kneeled down beside him to help.

Leaning backward, Grace squinted up at the cliffs above her. The rocks looked strange. She stood up to examine them more closely. Her fingers traced the smooth uniform ridges. Were they...tree trunk fossils? She stepped back to get a broader view. "Wow!" she exclaimed. There was a forest full of upright tree trunks encased in the cliff!

Wait 'til Dad sees this! The moment the thought sprung into her head, tears stung her eyes. He wouldn't see it, not ever. Her excitement at the fossil discovery evaporated as quickly as it had come. Grace pulled her dad's hat out of her pack. Careful to avoid looking at the stains on the brim, she switched it with her own, tugging it down over her eyes. It was loose, but she didn't adjust it.

Mai was staring at her. Grace quickly looked away. Rubbing away her tears, she wondered where Jeeter was. Where had he gone this time?

As if in answer to her silent question, he emerged from behind a huge boulder. "You guys aren't going to believe this," he said, a huge grin on his face. "Follow me!"

Fred tugged Mai toward where Jeeter was beckoning them. They scrambled over the terrain and out of sight around a corner. Alone, Grace dragged herself to her feet, her arm throbbing worse than ever. Her eyes were again drawn to the sea. It sounded like her wave machine. She was suddenly very tired. *If I lie down, will I float away?* she wondered to herself.

Grace reluctantly followed in the direction of her friends. As she rounded another outcropping, she stopped abruptly. There, in the middle of nowhere, was a big wooden wharf with two fishing boats and a huge yacht tied up to it.

"Wow!" Fred said, running toward the wharf. "I bet they have their own cook on a yacht like that. Maybe he'll make me a hamburger. I'm sooo hungry!" He stopped as he was about to step onto the wharf and turned to wave them on.

"Wait a minute," Mai said. "We don't know these people."

"Who cares?" Fred said, walking back toward his friends. "This is Cape Breton, not New York. You think they're the fish mafia or something?"

"Very funny, Freddo," Jeeter said. "But Mai has a point. They could be anybody."

"All I'm saying is that we have to be careful," Mai said. "Maybe we should check it out first."

"I'll go," Jeeter volunteered.

"Watch out," Mai warned. It seemed like she might follow him. But then Fred touched her arm and whispered something in her ear. Whatever he said, it convinced her to stay beside him. *That's a first*, Grace thought, *Mai listening to Fred?*

Jeeter walked slowly toward the yacht. It twisted slightly in the current, its long sleek side now visible.

Suddenly, Mai waved her arms frantically at Jeeter. "Jeeter, come back!" she rasped as loudly as she could. She pointed at the side of the yacht.

"Why?" he called back to her. "What's wrong?"

"Look at the name on the yacht! It's *Sandstar*!"

Chapter
26

JEETER MOTIONED TO HIS EAR AND SHOOK HIS HEAD. "I CAN'T hear you!"

"She said '*Sandstar*,'" Fred bellowed, cupping his hands to his mouth. "Never heard of it," he added, looking at Mai.

"Be quiet!" Mai said, yanking him backward. "Sandstar is the company that's dumping their toxic waste in the mines!" she explained.

"Oh, no!" Fred cried.

Vrrrbrubrbrubrub!

There was a low rumble, and a waft of smoke drifted from the back of the yacht.

"Hide!" Mai said frantically, pulling Fred and Grace down behind a boulder.

Grace poked her head back out. "Hide," she mouthed to Jeeter, pointing to the yacht. Jeeter dove behind a stack of crates just as two men appeared on the yacht's glistening white deck.

"It's almost high tide," the taller one said as he untied the mooring line. "We'll be able to get the rest of those barrels from the cave soon and that'll be the end of it."

"Just in time, too," his companion said. "That new strip mine will have workers and equipment crawling all over Point Aconi any day now."

"Yeah, we'll get this last batch to the old bootleg mine site in Florence that Stanley told us about and then there will be nothing left to find. They can dig 'til the cows come home and it won't matter."

The smaller one chuckled. "No one will ever find out that the incinerator can't handle all the waste. We'll get the full four hundred million from the contract and retire to some island. Heck, we can *buy* an island!"

Watching the pair from her hiding place, Grace gasped. Mai squeezed her hand.

The two men laughed.

"We'll get the barrels and come back here to wait. When it gets dark, we'll head to Florence."

"Where's that lazy bum Stanley, anyways? He was supposed to be here to give us a hand."

The tall man grunted. "He doesn't seem too fond of manual labour."

"I noticed that, too," the shorter one agreed. "Come on, we'd better get moving."

The two men disappeared inside the yacht. Moments later, the boat backed smoothly out of its mooring and cruised out of sight.

Grace couldn't believe it. It was true about Sandstar! And Rick Stanley *was* involved! She reached up and tugged her dad's hat down farther on her head.

"Let's check out those other two boats," Mai said to Fred. "Maybe there's a radio on board we can use to call for help."

"Jeeter," Grace called out as they walked onto the wharf. "They're gone. You can come out. Jeeter?" She poked her head behind the crates where he'd been hiding, but he'd disappeared again.

Cautiously, Grace, Mai, and Fred stepped onto the wharf and climbed aboard the boat closest to shore. The deck was faded and worn. The wheelhouse door was closed, its once-white surface covered in rust stains that had bled from the metal frame of its small round window. Green paint was flaked and peeling from the walls of the boat like the shedding skin of a snake. Only there wasn't anything new and shiny underneath.

"Do you think this bucket of bolts even runs anymore?" Fred asked, kicking a piece of an old life jacket.

"Well, let's check it quick and then we can try the other boat," Mai said. "One of them hopefully has a radio." She entered the wheelhouse, only to reappear almost instantly. "Nothing in there."

"Hey, this is weird," Fred said from over by the fish hold in the middle of the deck. He pointed to a thick chain and lock over the hold. It was shiny and new, and looked totally out of place with the rest of the boat.

"Maybe they've stored toxic waste in there too," Mai said, pulling on a lock of hair. "We should leave and see if there's a radio on the other boat."

"I'm going to check out what's down there," Fred said. He bent over an old toolbox wedged in a corner of the deck. Screwdrivers and pliers flew in all directions as he searched through the box, muttering to himself. "Aha! Right on the bottom!" He waved a rusty crowbar over his head like a trophy. "This should do it."

He stuck the crowbar between the links in the chain and leaned forward, trying to break it apart. The crowbar was no match for the new metal of the chain. Sweating, Fred flopped down on the deck. "Rats! It's not going to work."

"Good." Mai looked relieved.

"Um," Grace said, her curiosity getting the better of her, "what about the hinges on the other side? They look older, like the boat."

"That's just what I was thinking!" Fred said, leaping back to his feet with gusto.

Mai glanced over at Grace and rolled her eyes.

Fred wedged the crowbar under the first hinge and pulled. Crumbled pieces of rusty metal flew in all directions and the hinge snapped open. "Wow, that was easy," he said, popping the second one off and opening the hold.

"What's down there?" Grace asked. All three of them leaned over the gaping hole.

Grace shuddered. It reminded her of the cave they'd just escaped from.

They looked at one another hesitantly. No one seemed to want to be the first one to go in.

"Well, at least there's a ladder," Fred joked. The narrow metal rungs of the ladder were bent in spots and covered with the same rust-stained paint as the wheelhouse door.

"You go, Fred," Mai ordered. "It *was* your idea. I'll stand watch and look after Grace."

"Yeah, I guess it was my idea, huh?" Fred rubbed his hands together and stretched them over his head. He bent his knees as if warming up before a run. "All right, but if it's filled with gold—or money—I won't be sharing!" Flashing a toothy smile at them, he scrambled down the ladder and disappeared. "But I'll invite you over to swim in the pool in my millionaire mansion!" His words echoed up from below.

"Nut bar," Mai muttered. She kneeled at the edge of the hatch opening, looking down. "Are you all right?" she called.

"Yeah," Fred replied. "There's nothing down here."

"Then get back up here," Mai ordered.

"Wait, there's a door over in the corner," Fred called. "It looks like it's for a storage room or freezer or something like that."

"What's in it?" Mai asked.

"Can't tell," said Fred. "It's locked, too. Toss me down that crowbar and I'll try the hinges."

Mai dropped the crowbar into the hole. It clanged loudly on the floor below. All of a sudden light illuminated the hold. "Sweet!" Fred said. "There's power down here."

"That's strange," Mai said. "Why would there be power if there isn't even a rad—"

"I hear a voice! Someone's in there!" Fred hollered suddenly, cutting Mai off. "A *prisoner*!"

Chapter

27

POUNDING DRUMS BEAT PAINFULLY IN GRACE'S CHEST. HER HEAD was spinning as she grabbed the top rung of the ladder.

"Grace, your arm!" Mai's voice was full of concern. "Here, I'll help you."

Grace kept going. Sharp pains ripped up her arm to her shoulder.

"Over here," Fred called to Grace from the far side of the hold. "I can't get these hinges off. They aren't as rusted as the other ones. We'll need a screwdriver."

Grace raced to the door and pounded on it. "Who are you?" she cried. *Could it be him?*

"You won't be able to hear any words," Fred said. "The noise is too muffled by the door."

Grace pressed her ear to the cold metal door. She *could* hear noises inside. Someone was definitely in there.

"Here," Mai said, panting as she reached the bottom of the ladder. "I didn't know what kind you needed, so I brought everything I could find." She dumped an array of screwdrivers onto the floor.

Fred bent down, rummaged through the pile, and selected one with an x-shaped top and a blue handle. "This might work."

Grace paced back and forth as Fred worked on the hinges. "Fred, come on."

"I'm trying," he grunted.

Grace pulled at the lock and bolt. They were new too, like the one on the hatch up on deck. "Open!" she screamed, banging the lock with the heel of her hand. It didn't budge.

"Fred, hurry up!"

"Give me a break, Grace!" Fred wiped the sweat from his forehead with his sleeve. "I'm going as fast as I can!"

Grace banged at the door again, ignoring the pain in her arm.

"Stop it!" Mai said. "You'll hurt yourself even more."

"It could be my dad in there," Grace sobbed. "I have to get in. He could be *alive!*"

"What about a key?" Mai said.

"I couldn't find a key anywhere," Fred answered.

"That's because I have it," a voice said behind them.

All three of them whirled around. Rick Stanley stood at the foot of the ladder. Fred pulled Mai and Grace behind him and backed them against the door.

"You!" Grace said. "My dad's in that room, isn't he?" Her emotions were raging like a tornado inside her. "You *kidnapped* him?"

"Listen, I'm not the bad guy!" Rick said.

"You have to let me see him!" Grace's legs were wobbling.

"It's not that simple," Rick said, taking another step closer. He reached into one of his pockets. "It's the people I work with."

"Please!" Grace begged. "Open the door!" She moved toward Stanley but Mai gripped her arm and held her

back. "Mai, let me go!" she shouted.

"Grace, don't," Mai begged.

Grace struggled to escape Mai's hold. "He could be hurt. I have to see him."

"He's fine," Stanley said. "What do you think I am? A barbarian?" He took a step closer to Grace. "I'm the one who saved him. They would have killed him if I hadn't staged that car accident."

"What do you mean?" Grace said. As she spoke, she noticed something moving on the ladder above Stanley's head. Hiking-boot-clad feet slowly stepped onto the rungs. She recognized the cuffs of Jeeter's cargo pants.

"He found out about Sandstar dumping the toxic waste. He didn't get it—you can't mess with these guys." Stanley took his hand from his pocket.

Grace's stomach churned. She could taste vomit at the back of her throat. Did Stanley have a gun? Was he going to kill them?

Instead, Stanley pulled out a pack of cigarettes and stuck one between his lips. Relief flooded through Grace.

Stanley bent his head forward to light his cigarette. As the flame leapt from his lighter, Jeeter descended several more rungs on the ladder.

"Why are you asking all these questions?" Stanley asked, taking a drag on his cigarette. "You must know everything already. You sent me that note."

"What note?"

"Oh, please," he said. "Don't act all innocent! The note you put in my mailbox. *I know what you did to Jonathan Campbell*, it said. That's why I had to mess with your mother's car and get invited to dinner at your house. I had to try and see if there was any evidence in Jonathan's office about the dumping. I never found anything at the museum. I figured since you only sent that note now, after all this time, that you must have just found something. But then why didn't you go right to the police? That, I didn't get. What did you find? Photos? What?"

A note in his *mailbox?* "I don't know what you're talking about," Grace said. "I got a note in my locker saying it wasn't an accident and there was an envelope with your name on it."

Stanley looked as confused as Grace felt. *What was going on here?*

"Grace didn't send you the note," Jeeter growled from behind Stanley. "*I* did!"

Stanley spun around to face Jeeter. At that exact moment, Jeeter pounced on his chest, knocking him to the ground.

Grace watched in horror as Jeeter and Stanley fought, rolling around on the floor. Jeeter didn't stand a chance—Stanley was a lot bigger than him. She winced as Stanley punched Jeeter in the ribs.

We have to do something! Grace panicked.

As if he'd read her mind, Fred raced past her and jumped on top of Stanley. "Let him go, you creep!" he yelled.

Grace picked up the crowbar and tossed a screwdriver to Mai. "Let's go!" she hollered, racing over to the mass of arms and legs writhing around on the floor.

Mai swung her screwdriver.

"Ouch!" Fred cried. "Not me! Get the bad guy!" He grunted as Stanley elbowed him in the chest—hard. He rolled off to the side, trying to catch his breath.

Stanley lunged at Jeeter and grabbed him by the shirt. Jeeter took a wild swing at him, connecting with his jaw.

"Umph!" Stanley moaned, kicking Jeeter in the shin.

Fred got to his feet and charged back into the fray. But he tripped, accidentally knocking Jeeter to the ground.

Stanley pounced on top of Jeeter, pinning him to the floor. Jeeter was squirming and kicking, but he couldn't get free.

Holding her breath, Grace brought the crowbar down on Stanley's back as hard as she could.

CRACK!

"Uhhh," Stanley moaned. He went limp and rolled to the floor.

Jeeter pushed him away. "Thanks, guys," he said, panting and pressing a hand to his ribs.

"No problemo, Jeetman!" Fred said, helping Jeeter to his feet. The two boys exchanged a look of silent truce.

Grace bent down to search Stanley's pockets. "Here it is!" she said, holding up a key with trembling fingers.

She ran to the door and tried to unlock it. Her hands were shaking uncontrollably. "I can't get the key in the lock!" she cried.

"Let me help," Mai murmured beside her. She laid a steadying hand over Grace's and they turned the key together.

Chapter
28

THE LOCK CLICKED OPEN. GRACE HELD HER BREATH AND SLOWLY pushed the door inward.

Her dad was sitting on a small cot inside the storage room, his legs cuffed to a thick steel ring in the floor. His hair was ruffled and he was dressed in rumpled clothes that looked two sizes too big for him. The air in the room was stale and cold.

"Grace?" he croaked. He stretched his arms out toward her. "My word, is that really you? Am I dreaming?"

Grace raced to his side and threw her arms around him, ignoring the pain that flared in her injured arm. "Dad!" she cried. She buried her face in his chest.

"It's okay, Gracie," he soothed as he rocked her back and forth. "You found me...I thought I was buried for good."

Grace held him tighter. "I thought you were dead," she sobbed. He felt so thin and frail. She never wanted to let him go.

"I'll be okay now—thanks to you." He pried her gently away from him and looked up at her and Mai. "How did you kids find me?"

Grace stared up at her dad. His eyes were rimmed with red and his face looked pinched and pale. Uneven grey stubble covered his chin.

CRASH!

A loud bang came from outside the storage room. "Oh no you don't!" Fred yelled. There were more sounds of a scuffle and then Fred's sweaty face appeared in the doorway.

"Good news, Grace. Stanley woke up and he's not dead. So you're not a murderer." Fred smiled weakly, but he looked scared. "Don't worry, we've got him under wraps," he added, holding up a roll of duct tape. "Get it? Duct tape? Under *wraps*?"

"You're making jokes?" Mai shrieked. "He could be a murderer!"

Fred gulped and looked behind him, then gave a shaky thumbs-up.

Jeeter appeared beside him in the doorway. "Grace, we should get your dad out of those cuffs."

"Oh, right," Grace said. She reluctantly relinquished her grip on her dad's hand so she could pass the keys to Jeeter. Part of her thought he might be a dream and that he'd disappear if she let go.

"Sir, do you think you can walk?" Jeeter asked. "We should get to the other boat and get out of here in case those other men come back."

"What other men?" Grace's dad asked, frowning.

"The Sandstar people. They could come back any minute."

"They were here?" he asked. He took Jeeter's arm and tried to stand. He wavered and gripped Grace's shoulder for support.

"Take it easy, Jonathan," Jeeter said.

"I'm a bit dehydrated, I think," he said. "This has taken a toll on—Marcus, my word, what are you doing here, son?" he broke in, suddenly recognizing Jeeter. "I didn't recognize you without the long hair."

"Roger came out here to check on the tar ponds project. He had planned to come even before anything happened to you. He let me come, too—I wanted to see you again. But you had...disappeared...by the time we got here."

"Didn't he get my email about Rick Stanley? I hoped he might put two and two together and figure out what was going on."

Jeeter nodded. "He did, but you'd never said anything about Stanley working for Sandstar, just that he was acting strangely."

Grace's dad frowned. "I guess that makes sense. I didn't know for sure that there was any connection myself until I saw the barrels out at the PA4. But by then it was too late. Rick followed me there that day. He captured me and brought me here before I had a chance to tell anyone about the dumping."

"I tried to get Roger to look into your car crash," Jeeter explained. "But he wouldn't listen...he said he'd checked with the police and it was ruled an accident. But I...I couldn't let it go. I knew there was something wrong. So I tried to find out about Stanley on my own. Well, with Grace, I mean."

"Well, the important thing is that you found me," Grace's dad said, shaking his head. "I don't know how you managed to do it. I'm sure there is an explanation as to how you and Grace ended up here together. However, we have more pressing things to deal with at the moment. Has anyone contacted the police or the Coast Guard?"

"I tried to find a radio, sir," Jeeter said. "But Stanley showed up and I had to hide."

"Well, we'll have to get out of here as quickly as possible," Grace's dad said.

"Yeah," Grace added. "We don't want to be here when those Sandstar guys come back."

Fred and Jeeter duct-taped Stanley's wrists in front of him. At first, he refused to climb the ladder. But when Jeeter threatened to lock him up and leave him in the belly of the boat, he scurried up the ladder without another word of protest.

After Fred and Jeeter had tied Stanley up on deck, they returned to help Grace with her dad. It took a while to get him loaded onto the other boat as they had to stop every minute or so for him to rest. Eventually, they managed to get him aboard. Thankfully, there was no sign of the Sandstar yacht yet.

Grace's dad collapsed on a small bench on the deck. Sweat was running down his face and he was breathing fast. "My word," he gasped. He held a hand against his chest and closed his eyes. "You'd swear I had just climbed Mount Everest."

"Take it easy, Dad," Grace said.

He didn't answer. His face had gone white. Grace put her hand on his forehead. It was cold and clammy. "Mai, there's something wrong with him," Grace said. "He's unconscious!" Who knew what months of captivity and little food and drink had done to him?

Mai knelt down beside Grace's father and held his wrist. "His pulse is *really* fast," she said.

"What's wrong with him?" Grace asked.

"I don't know, Grace," Mai replied. "But I think he needs a doctor." She handed her bottle of water to Grace, and placed her jacket around Grace's dad's shoulders. "Let's keep him warm and see if he'll drink any water."

"Who knows how to drive?" Fred called from the door of the wheelhouse.

They all exchanged looks. Nobody spoke up.

Stanley snickered at them. "Not one of you knows how to drive a boat? This should be good. Do you have any idea what the currents are like around here?"

"Well if we drown, so do you!" Jeeter snarled.

"Fred, your dad owns a dive shop," Mai said. "Don't you know how?"

Fred shook his head. "My dad won't teach me. He says I have to wait 'til I'm older. Besides, he doesn't have time to show me—he's always either working or out diving."

"I've sailed a small boat on a lake before," Jeeter said. "It can't be that different, can it? I'll give it a try." He disappeared into the wheelhouse and a few seconds later the engine roared to life.

"Way to go, Jeeter!" Mai cheered.

"You'd better get us moving!" Fred said, pointing out to sea. The *Sandstar* was headed toward them—fast!

"I'm trying!" Jeeter called back.

Suddenly, the boat jolted backward.

"No, no, no!" Fred screamed. "The other way! You're going to hit the other—"

SMACK!

"...boat."

"Whoops!" Jeeter said. "Okay, okay, I think I've got it now."

The boat jerked forward. Grace almost fell off her seat on the bench. She lurched over to grab her dad and keep him from toppling onto the deck as the boat continued to pitch in place. "Jeeter!" she screamed.

"I don't know what's wrong!" he called back.

"We're still tied on!" Fred said. He raced to the side and grabbed the rope, fumbling to untie it.

"They're going to catch us!" Mai cried. She pointed at the *Sandstar* yacht, which had almost reached the wharf.

Fred pulled at the stubborn knot, but it wouldn't come undone. "I can't get it!" he cried.

WHOMP!

Grace chopped the rope in half with a small axe she'd found onboard. The axe sunk into the boat railing and the vibrations shot up Grace's arm, making her teeth chatter.

"Geez, Grace, you almost took my head off!" Fred said as he fell backward away from her.

"Yeah, but we're loose," she answered.

"Hold on!" Jeeter called back to them from the wheelhouse. The boat surged forward, quickly pulling away from the wharf. They picked up speed and veered left, away from the approaching yacht.

But they weren't fast enough. The *Sandstar* was right on their tail!

Chapter
29

JEETER RACED THE FISHING BOAT ALONG THE COAST, TRYING TO get as much of a lead on the *Sandstar* as possible. Waves crashed against the bow, showering the boat's occupants in cold ocean spray.

The *Sandstar* was getting closer. Grace could see the two men on the boat clearly. They were glaring at her with stone faces. She shuddered.

Grace rested a steadying hand on her dad's shoulder. He was lying on the bench, still unconscious. She'd wrapped her and Mai's jackets around him to keep him warm. "We have to do something to get rid of them," she said, looking back at the *Sandstar.*

Mai gaped at her with round eyes. "*Us?* Do something to *them?*"

"We're running away, that's something," Fred chimed in. The wind was whipping his sopping curls in a whirling helicopter around his head.

"But they're going to catch us," Grace said. "Then what?"

Mai and Fred stared silently back at her.

"Exactly," Grace said.

"There's nothing we can do," Fred said. "We don't have any weapons or anything." He gestured around the deck. "Hey, Jeetman!" he called toward the wheelhouse. "Speed this thing up!"

"I'm going as fast as I can!" came the harried reply.

"What if we could stop their boat somehow?" Grace said.

"How?" Mai asked, her forehead wrinkling as she rubbed her temples.

"I don't know," Grace replied, looking frantically around her. "Grab everything you can find!"

Mai nodded and immediately began rummaging in the storage boxes lining the side of the deck. She seemed relieved to have a task. Fred joined her, but all they found were a few fishing nets and a pile of old tools.

Grace sighed. What could they do with these? She reached down and picked up a rusted hammer. Frustrated, she turned to watch the approaching *Sandstar*. The man driving the boat smirked at her as the yacht edged closer.

"Leave us alone!" she screamed. Suddenly the hammer was flying through the air toward the yacht. Grace hadn't even realized she'd thrown it.

The driver swore and jerked the wheel. The hammer smacked against the bow and bounced up, hitting the windshield. Spiderweb cracks appeared on the glass.

Grace noticed that the yacht seemed to have slowed down.

"Try this," Mai said, handing her a screwdriver.

"Take that!" Fred said. He grabbed two wrenches and flung them at the boat.

Grace, Mai, and Fred pummelled the boat in a torrent of rusted and broken screwdrivers, wrenches, and hammers. Grace picked up the axe she'd just used to cut the rope and flung it with all her might. It hit the yacht with a loud smack. The windshield shattered and the men raised their arms protectively over their faces. The boat began swerving wildly.

But it didn't last long. Grace, Mai, and Fred were soon out of tools and the guys from Sandstar looked madder than ever.

They were done for!

"What about this?" Fred held up a lethal-looking claw with fishhooks all over it attached to a long fishing line.

Mai and Grace looked at each other. Grace shook her head. "You'll probably kill us with that thing."

"Then this is all we have left," Mai said, tugging at the edge of one of the fishing nets.

Frayed ends of braided twine didn't seem like much use against a giant yacht. Grace reached out and touched the wiry threads.

Well, they do *catch fish,* she thought. "Fred, you grab one end. Mai, you take the other. When I give you the signal, toss it back at the boat."

Mai looked confused. "What's that going to do?"

"I don't know, but it's all we've got." Grace sucked in a deep breath. They really needed something to go right for once. "I'll stand close to the railing and block the view. Maybe if they can't see you, they won't have time to get out of the way."

"Ohhhh," Fred said, nodding. "I get it!"

Grace crossed her fingers and whispered to herself, "Please let this work." She glanced at Mai and Fred. "On the count of three. One, two—"

"Uh, guys?" Jeeter's voice echoed from the wheelhouse. "We've got a problem."

The engine sputtered and Grace felt the boat slow down. What now?

"Three!" Fred called.

Grace whirled around to see the net sailing through the air. Everything seemed to be in slow motion. The men noticed the net too late. One shouted to the other as it fell over both of them.

The men were knocked down, and immediately the *Sandstar* slowed, then stopped. The men thrashed underneath the net, yelling and swearing. They were trapped!

Then suddenly the fishing boat's engine sputtered one last time and quit. Grace couldn't believe it. Now they were dead in the water, too!

They watched in horror as the *Sandstar* began drifting closer to them. What were they going to do now? That net wouldn't hold those guys forever.

"Grace, look!" Mai cried, pointing to a set of flashing lights out on the waves.

"Woohoo!" Fred cried. "The police!" He turned to Stanley. "Now you'll get what's coming to you!"

As the flashing lights came closer, Grace made out the red and white of two Coast Guard vessels speeding toward them. Within moments, one cruiser had pulled alongside the yacht. The two Sandstar men were still trapped and struggling beneath the net.

The second cruiser came up beside the fishing boat and tied on to it. A handful of Coast Guard officers swarmed over the side.

As she watched the officers boarding the fishing boat, Grace recognized a familiar face on the Coast Guard cruiser. She watched in horror as Stuckless stood up, took a step toward her, and leapt onto the fishing boat.

Suddenly, it didn't feel like a rescue at all. They'd traded one set of bad guys for another!

Chapter

30

"WHAT ARE *YOU* DOING HERE?" GRACE ASKED, BACKING AWAY FROM Stuckless.

"Grace, please don't look at me like I stole your puppy. I am *not* the bad guy."

"Could've fooled me," she said. "You're with him!" She pointed to Rick Stanley.

"I haven't a clue who that is," Stuckless said, barely glancing at Stanley. "I want to apologize if I've scared you."

"Scared me?" she said. "You followed me! You eavesdropped on us!"

She waited for him to deny it.

"I can explain," he said. He gestured to a tall man at his side. "My son's company, Breton Hauling Limited, almost went out of business waiting for those strip mining leases to come through. They kept getting delayed by your dad's protests."

Grace glanced up at Stuckless's son and gasped. He was wearing a hat that looked just like her dad's, but the letters on his were BHL, not DAL. "He was the one in the truck with you on Shore Road?" she asked, realization dawning on her.

Stuckless nodded. "You *were* there?" he asked. "I didn't see you."

"Strip mines?" Mai asked. "You mean you weren't dumping toxic waste? You don't work with Sandstar?"

Stuckless frowned. "Dumping waste? No, of course not! What we do is perfectly legal." He gestured to Grace, Fred, Mai, and Jeeter. "But you kids have been trespassing on company lands. I was sure you were up to something after I saw you at Halfway Road—more protests or other mischief. That would have been disastrous for my son's company."

"We're sorry, though," his son said gruffly. "We didn't mean to frighten you."

"So you decided to listen in on our walkie-talkie conversations?" Grace asked.

Stuckless turned red. "Ah, well...yes," he admitted, sheepishly holding up a walkie-talkie identical to Grace's. "I found this by one of the sinkholes. It's easy to pick up conversations if you find the same channel."

"Hey, that's mine!" Fred said, snatching his walkie-talkie from Stuckless.

Stuckless flushed even redder. "Again, my apologies," he said. "I was sure you were up to something. I had hoped that by listening in on your plans, we'd know ahead of time about any protests—and we'd be able to stop any vandalism."

"We weren't doing either of those things!" Grace said, outraged.

"I know that now," Stuckless said, holding up his hand. "But the other day when I saw you at the Halfway Road pit I thought you were spying for that protest group."

"We weren't," Grace said smugly. "If you really thought we were up to something, why didn't you tell my mother we were there?" she added.

Stuckless shrugged. "We'd started the strip mining a few days early. We weren't anxious to draw attention to that fact."

"But we didn't do anything at your strip mine sites," Grace said, confused. "Even today, when we were in the sinkhole, that was past the strip mines."

"I know," Stuckless said. "But who knows where those tunnels lead? When you didn't come back up from the sinkhole, I didn't know where you could have gone. I was looking for you out at the cliff by the lighthouse when I saw you below on the shore. When you boarded that boat, I had no idea what was happening. But as soon as I saw your father, I knew something was terribly wrong. I called the Coast Guard right away."

"*You* called the Coast Guard?" Grace asked. "Um, well, thanks." She felt weird saying it, especially after all that had happened.

Stuckless's son mumbled something to his father and the pair returned to the Coast Guard boat.

Grace watched as a handcuffed and scowling Rick Stanley was escorted to the Coast Guard boat along with the two men from Sandstar. She knelt beside her father, touching his cheek. "Dad, are you okay?" she asked.

His eyes fluttered open and he smiled up at her. Grace couldn't be sure, but his cheeks seemed to have some pink in them. She kissed him softly on the forehead.

Mai and Fred knelt down beside Grace and wrapped her in a group hug. "We did it," Grace said, feeling wet tears on her face. "We saved him."

"Grace?" Jeeter called. He was standing apart from everyone, leaning against the wheelhouse. "Can I talk to you?"

Grace stared at him for a minute, then nodded and followed him inside the wheelhouse. She retreated to the far corner, folding her arms across her chest. What could he possibly have to say to her after all the lies he'd told her?

"I need to explain things," he said. "So you can see my side."

"*Your* side?!" Grace spat. "You said your mother was dead! Who does that? You lied about everything—even your name!"

Jeeter stared out the window, his jaw clenched tight. "The thing about my mom didn't feel like a lie," he said. "Since the divorce...I never see her. She didn't just leave Roger. She abandoned me, too. All those things I said about how much it hurt...those were all true."

Even though she was angry, Grace felt a surge of sympathy for him.

"And Roger...I hardly even know him," he continued. "He works all the time. I feel like an orphan."

"I'm sorry, but what's that got to do with what you did to me?" Grace asked, her voice cold and sharp.

Jeeter looked at her, his eyes welling. "It's got *every-thing* to do with it! When Jonathan—your dad—came out to Alberta last year, he stayed with us. I got to spend time with him—he even took me out fossil hunting. It was the best time of my life."

Grace leaned against the wall. "I remember that...my dad used to write to me about this great kid, Marcus... *you!*" she said.

"He did?" Jeeter smiled through his tears. "He was so awesome! We went everywhere together. He was more of a father to me than Roger's ever been." He pulled a crumpled photo out of his pocket and handed it to her.

Grace looked down at the picture. It was a photo of her dad and Jeeter. They were both smiling, standing in a field. It looked a lot like the pictures she had of her and her dad together. She handed it back to him, not knowing what to say.

"Roger had been planning on coming here for some time. I begged to come, too. He was going to do a review of the tar ponds for Environment Canada. He and Jonathan used to talk about it all the time. The tar ponds are, like, the biggest environmental disaster in all North America. I think Roger thought it would be great for his career if he could find something wrong with the cleanup project. Jonathan was always saying the method they were using wouldn't work."

"Yeah," Grace nodded. "He was sure it would fail." She thought about the toxic waste. *He was right, too*, she thought to herself.

"So Roger and Jonathan were talking a lot on the phone about it, especially just before we came here. Roger was getting Jonathan's advice on how to do the review and what to look for. That last night, I picked up the phone—I wanted to say hi. I overheard Jonathan saying something about the trouble he was having with this Stanley guy that worked for him."

"Really?" Grace perked up.

"Yeah, and then we got here and your dad was gone." Jeeter shuddered. "I couldn't believe it. It felt like my own dad…. Anyway, I went to the police and told them to check Stanley out. But the police called Roger and I got into a whole pile of trouble."

"So then you changed your name and came after me!" Grace exclaimed.

"No," Jeeter said, looking horrified. "It wasn't like that. I had nowhere left to go. I thought maybe I could find something out by talking to you. Jeeter's my first name, by the way, but not what my dad calls me. I thought you'd recognize Marcus."

"I still don't know why you didn't just tell me," Grace said.

"Tell you what? I didn't have any proof. I even went to Stanley's house, watched him. I didn't see him doing anything suspicious. You never mentioned him in all the times we talked. Nothing. And then I started running out of time. Roger said there was nothing wrong with the tar ponds project, and that we'd be going back home as soon as school was over. I had to do something!"

A light bulb went off in Grace's head. "So you put that note in Stanley's mailbox at the same time you put the other one in my locker?"

Jeeter nodded. "I didn't know what else to do. By this point we'd become close and it was too late to tell you who I was—you would've freaked. But my plan worked. I knew Stanley was guilty as soon as I heard he'd gone to your house!"

"So the note in my dad's office....that was yours too, wasn't it?"

"Yeah. Your dad emailed Roger and mentioned that stuff about Stanley. It didn't seem like anything at the time. But right after...well, there was the accident..."

"Oh." Grace's head was spinning. She clenched her hands. Her knuckles brushed against the walkie-talkie strapped to her belt, triggering another thought. "So where did you get the walkie-talkie? Fred has yours."

"He has *one* of mine. When I bought them, they came in a set of two."

Grace frowned. "How come you didn't tell us that when we borrowed yours?"

"I could tell you were up to something—you're not a very good liar, Grace," Jeeter replied. "I wanted to know what was going on."

"You should have told me the truth," Grace said.

"The truth is I'm your friend, Grace," he said. "I was your friend all along. Please don't give up on me."

"I don't know, Jeeter," Grace said reluctantly. "I'll think about it."

Jeeter gave Grace a small, sad smile. "Okay. That's not what I was hoping for, but I'll take it."

Chapter
31

"MOM, ISN'T THAT ENOUGH BALLOONS?" GRACE ASKED. "I MEAN, my actual birthday was over three months ago!"

"Almost," her mother smiled, tying off another helium balloon and letting it float to the ceiling. A cloud of the coloured orbs swayed to and fro above them—a dancing rainbow ceiling.

Grace laughed. "The house is going to float away."

"Then let it! You never had a proper party and we have lots to celebrate."

It's now or never, Grace thought. Everyone would be arriving soon. "Mom, would you...? she started.

"What, sweetie?"

"Um," she looked down at her ugly chewed-off nails. "Could you, you know...?" Grace held up her hands.

"You want a *manicure*?" Her mom's mouth fell open and she let go of the balloon she was filling up. It flew crazily around the room.

"Just something so they're not as ugly," Grace said. "I can't stop biting them."

Her mom grabbed her in a tight hug. "I've got just the thing."

"Only one condition..." Grace said.

"What's that?" Her mom looked down into her eyes.

Grace smirked. "No ballerina pink."

"I think we can arrange that!" Her mom grabbed her hand and tugged her away to the manicure parlour in the sun porch.

*   *   *

Grace opened the door to find Fred and Mai standing on the front step.

"Happy fake birthday, Grace!" they sang.

"We got you a gift!" Fred said, holding up a brightly wrapped box.

"You bought it together?" Grace looked up to make sure the sky wasn't falling. "What are you, like, dating or something?" she joked.

Fred flushed so red Grace thought his head might pop off. So did Mai. They were like matching tomato plants.

"Let's get this party started!" Fred finally said, breaking the tension.

"What have you got up your sleeve?" Grace asked suspiciously.

"Charades," he said, holding up a stack of cue cards. "I wrote them all up already."

Mai rolled her eyes.

Later, as Fred contorted on the floor and acted out another wacky charade, Grace and the other partygoers exploded with laughter. No one could guess what he was supposed to be.

"I'm a fossil!" Fred moaned. "I can't believe you guys didn't get that one!"

"My word!" Grace's dad said, holding his side. "I can't take it anymore!"

Tears rolled down Grace's face as she hiccuped and laughed at the same time. It was the best party ever.

"I'd like to make a toast," Grace's dad said after they'd all gorged themselves on birthday cake. "To Gracie and her friends, the best fossil hunters ever. You brought me back, and I am forever grateful!"

Grace's mom had tears in her eyes as she held up her glass. "Cheers," she said, and they all clinked their glasses.

*   *   *

The next morning, after sleeping through the night without the help of her wave machine, Grace sat down at the computer to check her email. Along with the usual junk mail, there was a message from Jeeter:

To: fossilgirl@email.com
From: jeetman@email.com
Subject: Hey…

Happy birthday, Grace…belated, that is. ☺

I wish I could be there to celebrate with you and Jonathan. I hope he's feeling okay. I'm so sorry for everything.

Please write me back…I miss our late-night chats…and I miss you!

Jeeter (aka Marcus)

PS: Say hi to Fred and Mai for me.

Grace only hesitated a moment before she hit the reply button and told him all about her party.

By the time she was finished writing, the unmistak-
able scent of blueberry pancakes was wafting up to her.
She clicked send, then ran downstairs to help her dad
make the rest of the pancakes. By the time they were
done cooking, they'd used up every last blueberry from
the freezer.

*   *   *

"Dad, a little over the other way," Grace said, pointing
to her left.

"Ah, yes, I see it," he murmured. He turned toward her
and grinned.

Grace smiled back and relaxed in the rear seat of the
cabin cruiser. Her dad looked so good now that he was
out of the hospital. He'd suffered from severe dehydra-
tion, but there hadn't been any permanent damage. It
was a miracle, she knew.

"How long do we have this thing for?" Grace asked.
She ran her hand along the shiny white seat of the rented
boat. *What a great birthday present!* she thought.

"The entire weekend," her dad said. "So we can come
back again tomorrow if you want."

"I can't wait for you to see it," Grace said. "You'll never
believe it!"

They cruised past Little Table Island. Cormorants covered the high plateau. Seals lounged on the flat rocks
at the base, soaking up the sun and belting out loud
grunts and barks. It seemed like they were yelling at the
seagulls that screeched overhead.

Grace breathed in the salty air. "This is so beautiful,"
she murmered. She turned toward her mom, who was
bundled up in a bright orange life jacket. "You like it?"
she asked.

Her mother lifted her face toward the sun and sucked
in a deep breath. "It's amazing. I've never been on a boat

before—I was always too afraid since I can't swim." She grinned at Grace.

Grace could tell her mother was a little bit nervous. "Don't be scared," she said. She slid over and hugged her mom tight. "Dad and I will take care of you."

Her mom squeezed her back and placed a hand over Grace's. "I know I'm in capable hands with you two."

"Oh my word!" Grace's dad exclaimed suddenly. "I can't believe what I'm seeing!" His hands dropped off the controls and the boat slowed down, drifting gently in the current.

Grace bounced up and down in her seat as she stared at the cliffs in awe. "I know! Isn't it amazing?"

"What is that?" her mom asked. Her eyes were wide as she turned to Grace. "They sort of look like trees...but that can't be right...can it?"

"It sure can!" Grace exclaimed. She jumped to her feet and pointed at the tall trunks of the huge stone forest carved into the Point Aconi cliffs. The ridges on the trunks gleamed in the sunlight. "Did you know, Mom, that those trees are from the Carboniferous Period? That's three hundred million years ago—even before the dinosaurs!"

Her mom looked amazed. "Really?"

"It's true, Pat," Grace's dad said. "There have been rare discoveries of fossil forests like this in a few other parts of the world. But I've never seen anything like it with my own eyes." His gaze hadn't turned away from the site since they'd arrived. It seemed like he was mesmerized by it. "The erosion must have exposed it."

"Maybe this will get us heritage status—like Joggins," Grace said.

Her dad turned toward them, his eyes shimmering. "It will be great publicity for the museum. Perhaps we'll finally get some real government funding so we don't have to worry about being shut down every year."

"Maybe Mom can help us do it," Grace chimed in.

Her mom's mouth dropped open. "Me? But I thought this was something the two of you liked to do together. My dynamic duo." She looked self-conscious as she folded her hands in her lap, hiding her perfect nails.

Grace leaned over and pulled her mom's hands apart. "Dad and I got you a present," she said, pulling something out of her backpack. "Caving gloves!" She passed her mother a pair of brown leather gloves.

Grace's mom laughed, her eyes dancing. She slid her hands into the gloves. "A perfect fit!" she exclaimed. She held her gloved hand up.

Grace held up her own newly manicured hand beside her mother's gloved one. What a switch!

"Now there's a picture!" her mom said, clicking a shot with the digital camera.

"Dad and I may be your dynamic duo," Grace said, laughing. "But the three of us can be the three musketeers." She stood up and pointed to the stone forest. "Now let's get going. We've got fossil-hunting to do!"

Acknowledgements

To Mom, thanks for being my willing co-pilot as I dragged you all over the island! To Aunt Peg and her Master's in English, I'm grateful for the grammar tips. To the Writers' Federation of Nova Scotia, Jane Buss, and Norene Smiley, thanks for the workshops, the competition, and most of all the friendship. To my friends Rhonda and Sandy, thank you for being supportive readers of the drafts. To Caitlin, my editor, thanks for your keen eye and support. To the Cape Breton Fossil Centre, thanks for bringing the wonderful world of fossil treasures to us.

And lastly, to Cyndy and the rest of my writing pack, The Scribblers. It's hard to put into words how much you all mean to me. I know that I would not have continued on the long rocky road to achieve the dream without you. Thank you.